THE BRUMBACK LIBRARY
OF VAN WERT COUNTY
VAN WERT, OHIO

The Night of the Feathered Serpent

THE
NIGHT
OF THE
FEATHERED SERPENT

—⚬∿⚬—

Louise Bergstrom

AVALON BOOKS
THOMAS BOUREGY AND COMPANY, INC.
401 LAFAYETTE STREET
NEW YORK, NEW YORK 10003

JY

PRINTED IN THE UNITED STATES OF AMERICA
BY HADDON CRAFTSMEN, SCRANTON, PENNSYLVANIA

To my son-in-law, John Choate,
who loves the Mayan ruins as much as I do
L. B.

CHAPTER ONE

It was twilight when she arrived at Chichén Itzá—that dim, mysterious time when nature seems to draw back, gathering its forces against the encroaching night. The grounds of the old hotel were a jungle of tropical plantings, almost menacing in their lush, uncontrolled growth, and when Lori pulled into the parking lot, she stared in dismay at the old building.

The stucco walls, which she remembered as gleaming white, were now tinged an unhealthy shade of gray, redeemed only by the vividly colored bougainvillea vines that climbed them. But what disturbed her more than the unexpected shabbiness of the place were the stone serpent heads guarding the steps up to the entrance, their mouths gaping

1

open as though waiting to swallow an unwary victim. They looked somehow obscene in the dimming light. Had they been there before? Surely she would have remembered them.

The Feathered Serpent, she thought with a shiver: Kukulcan to the Mayans, Quetzalcoatl to the Aztecs—a vital if unwelcome part of that confused nightmare that she had come so far to try to clarify. It had been a long time since it had happened—twelve years—and she had been ten at the time. Naturally her memories would have faded to a certain extent, but the hotel did seem a lot shabbier than her memory of it. She had heard that the man who had owned it then had died and that his son had taken over. Perhaps he was not keeping it up as well as his father had.

Well, she thought, *things deteriorate rapidly in this damp climate. The building is probably much nicer inside.*

She climbed out of her rented car, got her two bags out of the trunk, and started toward the steps leading to the entrance. She paused a moment to read the faded lettering over the door: HOTEL KU-KULCAN. Perhaps it had been the son who had added the serpents. Could they be the real thing, salvaged from the unrestored ruins? More likely just copies.

She pictured the jungle stretching out around her, filled with the vast, secret, crumbling ruins of that lost, mysterious empire, and a shiver ran through her as though she had been brushed by a cold breath from the past. Perhaps it had been a mistake to come here—perhaps the answers she sought would remain as elusive as ever. Perhaps she did not even want to remember and it would be better to go away now while there was still time. The feeling of danger lurking there for her was very strong, like a jaguar of the jungle, waiting to leap—

Shaking herself mentally for such fantastic thoughts, she went on up the steps and through the big doors that were standing open. The hotel was much more attractive inside. The floor was of highly polished tiles; gaily upholstered wicker furniture was scattered around among the palms that grew in brightly colored pots. There were some excellent paintings of the ruins on the walls.

Lori set down her bags and approached the desk, behind which sat a very attractive young woman wearing one of the native Yucatán dresses. Her gleaming black hair was done in a simple coiffure, and her large eyes were very dark. There was a gold chain around her neck, from which hung a curious little figure—no doubt one of the Mayan gods. The woman looked up with a friendly smile at Lori's approach.

"Good evening," Lori said. "My name is Lori Cahill and I have a reservation."

The young woman consulted her records. "Yes, Miss Cahill, that is correct. Cottage number six."

She spoke in precise although accented English. Convent-educated most likely, Lori thought.

She handed Lori a card to fill out, and before she started working on it, Lori took a casual glance around the lobby, which had appeared almost deserted when she'd come in. Now she saw that over in a corner, watching her with interested blue eyes, was an elderly lady in a violently flowered shift. Curly white hair piled haphazardly on her head, and she held a fat pug dog whose features curiously resembled her own. Lori smiled at her, and she smiled back with a little wave.

Lori was just finishing the card when a man came out of the office behind the desk. He was tall and very thin, probably in his early thirties, with a long, sad, Spanish face and a drooping mustache— a Don Quixote type, Lori thought.

"Welcome to the Hotel Kukulcan," he said, giving her a melancholy smile. "I am Julian Neri, the owner of the hotel." He spoke with practically no accent. "I will show you to your cottage. I understand you wanted the one where you stayed with your father some years ago."

"Yes, that's right. Number six. He was one of the archaeologists working on the restorations."

"Ah, yes. You probably don't remember me, Miss Cahill, but I was home for my spring vacation—I went to the University of Miami at the time —and I remember you. I thought your father was a very fine man. It was an honor to have him and his group in our hotel. I was sorry to hear of his death. We have both lost our fathers since that year." He continued to gaze at Lori mournfully, and she said, "Yes. Of course my memory of that week isn't very clear now. . . ."

She waited, wondering if he would make some reference to the curious events that had occurred then, but apparently he did not intend to. He picked up her bags and started off, saying, "Fortunately I was able to give you the same cottage, so if you will just follow me. . . . We're rather shorthanded just now. All the hotels were filled to capacity last week for the serpent ceremony, but most of the tourists have gone now, and some of our help are on vacation."

She followed him toward the rear doors, which led out onto a terrace. They were sliding glass doors, now standing open, and as she turned she caught a glimpse of sudden movement, as though someone who had been standing there had hurried away. One of the other guests, no doubt, she thought, as they went on out to the terrace.

It was a wide terrace of the polished tiles one sees everywhere in Mexico, and it was furnished with a number of small tables, where a few guests were already seated having the Mexican equivalent of a happy hour. Beyond this was a large pond surrounded by a junglelike garden, as lushly overgrown as the rest of the grounds. In the center of the pond was a fountain splashing away, and a tiled path circled off around the pond.

They went down the broad steps from the terrace, taking the left-hand branch of the path. When they were closer to the fountain, Lori noticed that there was an odd-looking statue in the center of it, and she paused to study it. The figure was that of a man in ancient Mayan attire leaning back on his elbows, his knees bent and his head turned to one side. On his lap he held a bowl from which the water was spouting. There was a strange, blank expression on his broad face. Something stirred in Lori's memory, and she felt a vague uneasiness.

"Isn't there a figure like that in the ruins?" she asked.

"Yes, that is a Chac-Mool from the Toltec era. There is a fine example of one at the Temple of the Warriors, which is probably what you remember."

She had been away from archaeology for a long time, but some of what her father had taught her was starting to come back. "It was used for something rather nasty, wasn't it?" she said. "Isn't that the bowl where they put the heart of the sacrificial victim after tearing it out of the body?"

"So they say." He seemed reluctant to discuss it. His expression was closed, remote.

"No wonder he has his head turned away!" Lori said dryly.

Julian's expression became even more melancholy. "It was a Toltec custom," he explained.

"Originally the Mayans did not use human sacrifices."

Oh, of course, Lori thought. *They just got in with a bad crowd.* But she didn't want to offend him; perhaps he had Mayan blood.

"An offering to the sun god," she said. "Of course that's just a replica—"

"I'm afraid not. When the hotel was built by my grandfather a long time ago, he brought in many things from the unrestored ruins in the jungles behind us. That statue was broken in several places, but he hauled it in, put it back together, and made a fountain out of it."

"I seem to remember being afraid of it—especially at night," Lori mused. "I expected it to come sneaking over to our cottage—after my heart!"

Julian smiled faintly. "You were an imaginative child, as I recall—fond of making up wild stories. There was that incident involving one of the college boys working for your father—didn't he disappear, and you were hurt some way and claimed you'd seen him murdered? Only, he wasn't, of course. He'd just run off and hitched a ride to South America on somebody's yacht."

Lori stared at him. So he did remember, after all. "How do you know he really went to South America?" she demanded. "Did anyone ever hear from him?"

"I would have no way of knowing that," he said, shrugging, "but he did leave a note saying he was going, and his car was found near the docks in Cancun. I remember that early one morning you were found out on the road wandering around in your pajamas, with your head all bloody from a cut, and you told some wild tale about seeing Erik murdered in the pyramid. But when the police went to look, there wasn't any pyramid there, only part of a ruined building, and certainly no body. Your father said you'd probably just had a nightmare and walked in your sleep. You did that sometimes. Then your mother came and took you home, and that was the end of that."

Lori didn't try to argue with him. What he said was true enough—except that she knew it had not been a nightmare. The nightmares had come later. . . .

"Well," he said, picking up her bags again, "we'd better get you to your cottage. I'm sure you're tired after your long flight." He started off along the path, and Lori followed him.

The cottages were set in a semicircle at the far side of the pond. They were imitation thatched-roof huts, but they had screened porches and were completely modern inside. There were only six of them, and the one Julian took Lori to was the last one on the left. They went up on the porch, and Julian set down her bags and unlocked the door.

Inside there was one big room with a double bed, a table and chairs, and a studio couch on one side. At the back was a tiny kitchenette and a bathroom.

The furniture looked new to Lori. It seemed to her that she'd had only a cot to sleep on and that the furniture had been shabbier.

"Have you bought new furniture since I was here?" she asked.

"Yes, all the cottages had to be done over. My father was not well the last few years of his life and allowed the place to go a bit to seed. I've been making what improvements I can as time and money permit. There is still a great deal to be done, especially on the outside."

"There are more hotels here than there used to be too," she commented. "Does the competition bother you?"

"Not really. There are more tourists than ever coming here, and I get my share of the business." He looked around the room. "If there is anything you need, call the desk and I will see that you get it. Dinner is served from seven to ten."

"Thank you, Julian. I'll be over later."

He gave her his mournful smile and went away.

Lori stood there, gazing around the room, trying to recapture the feelings she'd had as a very young girl. In spite of the new furniture, the place was still quite the way she remembered it. How thrilled she had been that Easter vacation, flying down from Chicago all by herself to stay with her father. And how fascinated she had been with the ruins and the work the men were doing. She'd learned a lot too. Her father had lectured her constantly on the Mayan culture and history. It had all been wonderful until that strange night— Well, no use brooding about it now. At least she was here and could try to get closer to the truth. Perhaps she could even find the elusive pyramid.

She unpacked her clothes, took a quick shower, and put on a light cotton shift, more suitable to the tropical climate than the heavy jeans she'd worn on the plane. Of course it had still been quite cold in Chicago when she'd left, since it was only the last week of March.

With a sigh, she sat down on the one comfortable chair and again looked around the room. There was a dead cricket under the table. Oh, well, better a cricket than a tarantula. She remembered seeing a few of those in the jungle when she was here before.

It had been a tiring two days. First the flight from Chicago to Miami, then the late afternoon flight to Mérida. A night spent at a hotel in the city, then a bus tour of Mérida the following morning, and finally the drive in the rented car to Chichén Itzá.

It hadn't been a very interesting drive. The Yucatán peninsula probably had about the dreariest scenery in all of Mexico, even counting the deserts. It was mostly scrubby brambles and thorns, dotted with little villages where the natives lived in round, thatched-roof huts just as they had for hundreds of years.

It was very dark now, with the sudden darkness

that descends in the tropics when the sun goes down. She thought of the recurring nightmare that had troubled her sleep for so many years—ever since the night that she had come to think of as The Night of the Feathered Serpent—and wondered again if she had really seen Erik killed. Would she ever know?

Something drew her eyes up to the uncurtained window across the room, some slight movement in the darkness of the dense shrubbery that grew close to the cottage on that side. She stared out into that darkness intently, almost holding her breath. Then a face appeared against the screen, wavering uncertainly: a strange face, somehow not quite human, with blank, staring eyes that seemed to see her and yet not see her. . . .

CHAPTER TWO

Lori let out a strangled scream and ran for the door. As she flung open the screen and started down the steps, she collided with a man who had just started to mount them. More frightened than ever, she began to pummel him with her fists when he grabbed her arms to keep her from falling.

"Let me go!" she gasped.

"Hey there," he said soothingly, releasing her and backing off a step. "Where's the fire?"

She looked up at him, and by the light of a security lamp near the pond, she was reassured by his wryly amused smile and friendly hazel eyes. About the same age as Julian, he too was tall and thin,

12

with pleasantly rugged features and thick brown hair.

"A face!" she explained wildly. "A terrible face looking in my window! It might have been the Chac-Mool!"

He looked a bit startled, but promptly ran off around the cottage to check the window she had indicated. He made a complete circuit and came back.

"There's nothing there now. What exactly was it you saw?"

She tried to describe it. "It had the face of the Chac-Mool," she insisted. "You know, that statue in the fountain that holds a plate on his belly where he puts the hearts of his victims."

He grinned. "If it's interested only in hearts, why would it peer in your window?"

"Maybe it wants mine!"

"Can't say I blame him. Probably just some Peeping Tom."

"It wasn't a human face. It had the blank, inhuman expression of the Chac-Mool."

"Interesting—a Peeping Tom Chac-Mool. What will they think of next?"

She could see that he wasn't going to take her seriously.

"What were you doing on my doorstep, anyway?" she demanded.

"I saw you arrive with Julian. I just thought I'd

be neighborly and ask you over to the terrace for a drink. After what happened, you look like you need one. My name is Brian McDouglas, and I'm in the cottage next door."

He was regarding her with a flattering expression, and now that she was looking at him as a man and not as an invader, Lori liked what she saw. Definitely masculine but not macho, nice sense of humor.

"Lori Cahill," she replied. "I'll take you up on that offer."

When they reached the terrace, there was still a smattering of other guests occupying the little tables, although the majority had gone in to dinner. They found a spot off in a corner next to the railing, with the fountain splashing nearby. Lori gave the Chac-Mool an uneasy glance. He looked quite settled in, so she decided he couldn't have been the one at her window.

The waitress came over to them, and they ordered margaritas. The waitresses were all pretty young women wearing the native costume of the Yucatán called a *huipil,* a white cotton shift trimmed at the neckline with pink, orange, and red flowers. This was worn over a lace-trimmed petticoat that extended a few inches below the hem of the shift, showing off the fancy trim.

Lori had seen women wearing them even to do dirty labor in the villages she had driven through, and they had always appeared neat and clean—not an easy accomplishment when one considered that they washed all their clothes by hand in a river.

"I love those dresses," she remarked. "Maybe I'll buy myself one."

"You'd be adorable in it," Brian assured her. "You're very lovely, Lori, with that long silver hair and those silver eyes, like something out of a fairy tale. Where did you get a combination like that?"

"They were having a sale at Marshall Field's," she said. "But really, Brian, my hair isn't silver, just ash-blond, and my eyes are light gray."

"Silver," he said stubbornly, "and you can't make me believe you're not a princess in disguise."

Lori smiled. "A violinist friend once told me that I looked as though I should be walking through a misty forest leading a unicorn."

"Exactly. And now it seems you are being pursued by evil demons. We'll have to do something about that."

The waitress brought their drinks, and Brian lifted his glass.

"To unicorns," he said, "and fairy princesses."

It seemed to Lori as though she had known Brian a long time, and they fell into easy conversation. She told him about her flight to Mérida from Chicago and the lonely drive through the bleak Yucatán countryside. Brian said that he published a monthly travel magazine and had come down to photograph the serpent ceremonies; he had driven over the same route the week before.

"What impressed me most," she said, "was the lack of furniture in the native huts. They didn't even seem to have any beds."

"Oh," he said, "they sleep in hammocks that they put away in the daytime. I understand that they raise a special sort of hairless dog here called the xoloizouintle, that sleeps with them on cold nights. When it's especially cold, they just pull up another xoloizouintle. That's what is known as a two-dog night."

"Brian," she said, "did anyone ever tell you that you are a nut?"

"Come now, I'm only giving you a few historical facts. And speaking of facts, would you mind telling me just why you came down here all alone? It seems rather unusual—"

Lori hesitated. She wasn't quite ready to tell him the whole truth. Not yet.

"I was here twelve years ago with my father," she said. "He was an archaeologist, here with a team working on the restoration. I came down on my spring break. He died a few years after that, and I just wanted to see the place again. You might call it a sentimental pilgrimage."

"Was your mother with you?"

"No, she's a musician and couldn't get away, and anyway she hated life at the digs. They had an odd sort of marriage, I suppose, separated so much, but it seemed to work for them. He was home part of the time, of course, working at the museum."

"What sort of musician is your mother?"

"A flutist. Isn't that an awful word? Mother says it makes her feel like an old woman with dyspepsia. She's with the Chicago Symphony. So is my step-father—he plays second violin. It's a more sensible marriage than her first; at least they're always together."

"And what do you do?"

"I'm a flute player too. Mother started me on it when I was quite young. For a while I wanted to be an archaeologist like my father, but then he died and I was constantly surrounded by music and musicians, so I gave in to it. I love music."

"Are you with an orchestra too?"

"At the moment I'm out of work, but I'm hoping to get into the Civic Opera orchestra next fall. For the past couple of years—since I graduated from the Conservatory—I was with a little ensemble that played dinner music at big hotels—you know, Strauss, Friml, Herbert, that sort of thing. Very genteel. This past winter we had an engagement on a cruise ship in the Caribbean."

"Sounds like fun."

"Oh, it was. But then we finally broke up and I didn't mind. It's time I got into more serious work, anyway. But that's enough about me. Tell me about your magazine and where you and it live when you're at home."

"A little coastal town in Oregon, where I was born," he explained. "The magazine is called *The*

Magic Carpet, and it runs articles on low-budget places of interest. Usually we buy free-lance material, but I do some articles myself. I was interested in the serpent ceremony—that's why I came here. I was about ready to leave—but now I think I'll hang around awhile if I can keep the cottage."

She regarded him thoughtfully. "Do you live alone?" she asked. "Forgive my curiosity, but it's something I always check out."

"I don't blame you. Yes, I live alone—more or less. When my father retired, he and Mother wanted a warmer climate, so they turned their house over to me and bought a condo in California. However, they come back for the months of July and August. Otherwise, it's just me and old Kilmer."

"Kilmer?"

"Yes, my dog. Loves trees, you know. What about you? You must meet a lot of fascinating men, traveling around in such glamorous circles."

She made a little face. "Naturally. Unfortunately, most of them turn out to be jerks. That's why I got my black belt in karate."

As they sat there, sipping their drinks and smiling into each others eyes, Lori suddenly became aware that she was being watched. Having spent a good many years being stared at by crowds of strangers, she had developed a certain sensitivity to the emotions of the people around her. Things like lust and admiration were easy to identify, but now what she sensed was a concentration of attention.

. Carefully she looked around the terrace. There was a group of obviously retired couples, probably a tour group, who had pulled several tables together and were engaged in spirited conversation. Over in a far corner were two men, one old, probably in his sixties, with a brown, weather-beaten face, a bald head with just a fringe of white hair, and sharp blue eyes.

The other man was young, and so beautiful that Lori couldn't help but give a little gasp of admiration. He was slender and well built, but it was his face that caught her attention—the face of a medieval angel, with high cheekbones, full, sensuous lips, a crop of short, bronze curls that covered his head like a cap, and soulful dark eyes. It was he who was staring at her with such an air of curious concentration.

Brian followed the direction of her gaze.

"Hey, no fair!" he cried indignantly. "I saw you first."

Lori frowned slightly. "I wonder who he is."

"No doubt you'll find out."

Seeing them looking at him, the young man turned back to his companion.

"He looks as though he just stepped out of a painting by an old master," Lori said.

"Then I wish he'd step back in," Brian muttered.

"Lori, you ought to realize that no man who looks like that can be trusted an inch."

"Oh, I don't know. I've had just as much trouble with the ugly ones. But don't worry, Brian. I didn't care for his vibes."

Brian looked happier. "You didn't? What's wrong with them?"

"I'm not sure. Anyway, let's go in and get something to eat. I'm starved."

They went inside to the dining room. Here the dinners were served by waiters also in native costumes; the pretty girls were clearing the tables. Lori studied the menu and decided on something called chicken Yucatán, which turned out to be very good, glazed with a spicy-sweet tomato sauce. There were French fries and mixed vegetables with it and something that looked like mashed black beans.

"That's called refried beans back in the States," Brian told her. "They serve them with everything here. Not bad."

Later, when they had had their coffee, they went back to the terrace. Julian came over to them.

"Did you enjoy your dinner?" he asked.

"Very much," Lori assured him.

"We are noted for our food. Many people come here for dinner from the larger hotels."

"I can see why," Brian said. "I won't hesitate to recommend your hotel in my article."

Julian smiled a bit less mournfully than usual.

"Have you seen our swimming pool?" he asked Lori.

"I didn't know you had one," she replied. "There wasn't one when I was here before. Where is it?"

"Down those stairs at the right end of the terrace. Come, I'll show you."

"If you'll excuse me for a bit," Brian said, "I have to call my assistant editor back home. I'll see you later, Lori."

He went off on his errand, and Julian and Lori strolled toward the steps. The ground sloped there, and there were a dozen or so stone steps leading down into the garden. A tiled path led off through the thick vegetation, and as they walked along it, Lori wondered if she should tell Julian about the face at her window. She decided against it—there wasn't much he could do about it now.

They soon came out into a clearing where a beautiful pool lay shimmering under the colored lights strung in the trees that surrounded it. There was a tiled patio around the pool, with a number of little metal tables and chairs, but at the moment the place was completely deserted. A half-moon overhead gave additional glamour to the scene.

"How lovely!" she exclaimed. "I'll certainly make use of it tomorrow."

"It was just put in this year," Julian said proudly. "My father always said we didn't need one, but with all the new hotels going up, I felt that I must make improvements in order to compete."

"How long have you been running the hotel?" she asked.

"My father died six years ago." He was gazing at the pool with a gloomy expression. "I don't really care for pools myself," he murmured. "I'm afraid of water, because of the nightmares. . . ."

Nightmares? Lori felt a wave of excitement. Was he another victim of them—and could there be a connection with her own?

"What sort of nightmares?" she asked tensely.

He shook his head. "It's something I don't like to talk about."

She could understand that; she seldom mentioned her own.

"I don't mean to pry," she said, "but I'm really interested. I've made a study of them."

"You have?" He looked up with a puzzled frown. "Why?"

"Because I've been troubled by one myself."

"Oh, yes. Like the night you dreamed you saw Erik being murdered by a feathered serpent. Well, mine are about the *cenote*—the sacred spring, you know. Do you remember it?"

"Very well. Aren't there two of them? I wasn't supposed to go there alone, but I used to sneak over to explore when my father was working."

"Yes, there are two of them. One was for drinking water, and they don't take tourists there. Of course you can go on your own, but most tourists are interested only in the one where the sacrifices were made. That's the one I dream about."

"What is your dream?"

"As you may know, the sacred well is located in more or less a straight line from the great Temple of Kukulcan—"

"The one the guidebooks refer to as the Castle?"

"Yes, but it was never a castle, just a temple. They would hold ceremonies on top of it, and then the procession would walk along the road to the *cenote* with the sacrificial victims. In my nightmare I am in that procession, being led along with a group of other children. We are naked and painted blue, the sacred color of the Mayans. I can see it so plainly—the marvelous feathered costumes of the priests and their attendants and the musicians. . . . Then there is the chanting—the terrible chanting. I keep looking around for my mother, but when I finally locate her, she looks at me as though she doesn't know me. That is the worst part of all. I wake up in a cold sweat."

"It sounds dreadful," Lori sympathized. "Did they really throw children in the *cenote?* I thought it was virgins."

"Oh, many children. For the rain god, Chac. Sometimes there were droughts that ruined the crops. It wasn't really virgins they sacrificed, but that's what pleases the tourists to hear.

"Besides the children they would throw in prisoners, slaves, anybody they chose. Divers have found bones of thousands in there, as well as fabulous treasures: gold, jade, emeralds, turquoise, and so on. Of course, those things aren't native to the Yucatán—it has nothing—but traders came here from all over to make offerings to the gods."

"In your nightmare, do you ever actually get thrown into the spring?"

"No. It always stops short of that, sometimes at the edge of the platform from which the victims were thrown. I've always had the feeling that if I ever actually went into the *cenote* in my dream, I would never wake up."

She couldn't repress a shiver at the melancholy resignation on his face.

"Did the victim always drown?" she asked.

"Not always, but usually. They threw them in at sunrise, and if they survived until noon, they'd haul them out to learn the god's secrets."

"Why do you think you have this nightmare, Julian?" she asked. "When you were a child did someone tell you stories about those ancient rites?"

"Yes, my grandfather—my mother's father—who was of Mayan blood. He lived nearby in a village that is abandoned now, and I spent a lot of time with him."

"Do you think it might be his stories that gave you the nightmare?"

Julian shrugged. "That's the logical explanation, of course. But I have always believed that once I actually was one of those children who died in the *cenote*."

Lori stared at him, intrigued by the idea. "Then I'm surprised you stay here. I should think you'd want to go far away to escape the nightmare."

"One cannot escape his destiny," he replied with dignity. "Anyway, where would I go? This is my home, my career. Well—I must get back to the hotel."

When he had gone, Lori continued to stand there gazing at the pool. She would go to take a look at the *cenote* tomorrow, she decided. It didn't seem to have any connection with her own problem, but it interested her. She would return to all the places she had known before. Perhaps they would help her remember the missing parts.

Of course, the most important thing of all would be to find the pyramid hidden in the jungle. It had to be there, even though she had been unable to lead the police to it and everyone thought it was just a nightmare. It was not likely that any more restoration had been done in that area, so it would still be there, buried in vegetation.

The sound of approaching footsteps startled her, and she turned to see Brian coming down the steps to the pool.

"Beautiful spot, isn't it?" he said.

She nodded. "Lovely."

He gave her a sharp glance. "What's the matter?

You look so solemn. Has the Chac-Mool been after you again?"

She smiled. "No, nothing like that. But I had a very interesting conversation with Julian just now. He seemed to be in a mood to confide in me."

"It's those big, trusting, silver eyes of yours, m'dear. What did he confide to make you so thoughtful?"

Lori hesitated. Julian hadn't asked her not to tell anyone about his dream, so she didn't think he'd mind if she discussed it with Brian. She repeated what he had said about his strange nightmares.

"Do you think he really could have lived that experience long ago?" she asked.

"Who knows? This is such a strange place, you can believe almost anything. On the other hand, the dreams could have been the result of the stories told by his grandfather. You know how children are. Didn't you ever dream about some of the frightening stories you heard?"

"But apparently he still gets the dream at times," she said, and she was tempted to tell him of her own nightmare. *Soon,* she thought, *but not quite yet.* She hadn't known him long enough.

They walked slowly back toward the cottages.

"Tomorrow," she told him, "I'd like to lay in a few supplies. Not that I intend to do any real cooking, but since there is a little hot plate in my kitchenette, I could at least make coffee when I want it."

"That's what I've been doing," Brian replied. "I

like to fix my own breakfast occasionally, and I like coffee permanently on tap. There's a little grocery down the road. I'll take you there in the morning."

From the pool area, it was necessary to walk past all the other cottages to reach theirs.

"When I was here before," Lori said as they walked, "the cottages were all occupied by the archaeologists and their families. That is, those who brought their families. And the student workers, of course."

"Was your father in charge of the project?"

"Yes. There were six student workers and a couple of other archaeologists as I recall. It's all rather hazy now. Do you know the people renting the cottages now?"

"Only to speak to. I wouldn't say I was exactly chummy with any of them. Lover Boy, the fellow you admired on the terrace, is in this first one—he paints or something. In two and three are a couple of elderly ladies. One is a retired teacher; the other an odd little character with a pug dog, who is supposed to be a medium, believe it or not. The lady, I mean, not the dog."

"She must be the one I saw in the lobby when I arrived. What about the one next to yours?"

"Dr. Parker, a retired archaeologist who says he's writing a book."

At Cottage 3 a porch light was on, and Lori saw the Pug Lady and another about the same age sitting at a little table playing cards. The pug dog was sitting on the steps and gave them a bored look and a faint woof as they went by. The ladies gave them a friendly wave.

"The lady with the dog looks vaguely familiar," Lori said. "I wonder if she was here twelve years ago."

"Could be. Julian said some of the guests have been coming for years." They had reached the steps of Cottage 6, and Brian looked down at her a bit quizzically.

"Are you sure you'll be all right?" he asked. "I mean, you aren't afraid someone is lurking around?"

"What would you do about it if I *were* afraid?" she asked, smiling up at him.

"Sleep on your couch or something, I guess."

"That would be silly. You're right next door. I'll yell if anything happens, and you can come running."

"I certainly will." He took her hands and continued to gaze down at her with a bemused smile. "I never thought it could hit me so hard and so fast," he murmured.

The way he was looking at her sent a tremor through her, and she realized that she didn't really want him to leave her at all. But that wouldn't do —she had to keep her wits about her if she were to accomplish what she'd come here to do. So she removed her hands from his and went up a step toward the screen door.

"Don't worry," he said. "I won't inflict my emotions on you now, my beautiful little flutist. I can see that you're not in the mood. But just tell me this—is there anyone anywhere you're seriously involved with? As you said yourself, I like to check these things out."

She went up another step, reluctantly. "No, Brian," she said. "No one special."

"Good!" They were about on a level now, and he leaned over and gave her a chaste kiss on the brow. "Good night, princess. Let me know when you want to go over for breakfast, and then we can visit the ruins together."

She went slowly on into the cottage. When she was ready for bed, she took a paperback out of her flight bag—she never traveled without a good supply of them—and lay down on the bed. She always read herself to sleep, but tonight she couldn't seem to concentrate. She lay there with the book on her chest, staring at the window. The drapes were closed now, but she was still very conscious of the dark jungle stretching away behind the cottages. Had there really been a face out there? Yes, there had been, although it seemed so inexplicable.

There was no air-conditioning in the cottages, only ceiling fans, so she had to keep the windows open. Of course they had screens, but that wouldn't keep out anything but insects. There seemed to be a lot of crickets around; she could hear them singing in the surrounding shrubbery. There were also night birds of some sort. Back in Chicago it had been cold, with remnants of snow on the ground, but here it was like summer.

Her thoughts grew confused as the edges of sleep crept over her. What a strange place this was, she mused. All those unseen ruins out there still vibrating with ancient terrors and awful gods that nobody now really understood. The Chac-Mool holding the still-throbbing heart—the pool where innocent children were drowned—the terrible serpent sun-god, Kukulcan, in whose name all manner of unspeakable things were done. . . .

She was just drifting off into an uneasy slumber when a sound outside the screen door on the porch brought her back to awareness. The screen was latched, but she had left the cottage door open for better ventilation. With all the bushes around, it had seemed private enough. She lay there, barely breathing, listening. It came again: a soft sound, as though something were moving around out there, rubbing against the screen. There was a curious snuffling sound—

What was it? Some animal from the jungle? The Chac-Mool? She sat up and shook her head to clear it of such fuzzy nonsense. Slowly she lowered her feet to the floor and stood up, all senses alert now. Maybe if she went to the screen door, she would frighten it away. At least she could see what it was. It might be some small, nonthreatening animal.

Cautiously she walked out onto the little porch.

She could hear the splash of the fountain nearby and the shrilling of the crickets. Something rustled in the bushes off to her right. If it had been an animal, perhaps her approach had frightened it away. She reached the screen door and peered through it. The colored lights had been turned off around the pool now, but there was still a faint glow from the yellow security lights set at intervals along the path. She thought she saw a faint shadow move along the walk.

Three wooden steps led down to the tiled path that led through the garden around the pond and back to the hotel. She unlatched the screen door, opened it, and stepped outside. She was uneasy, but certainly not terrified. If there was an animal around, she wanted to find out what it was. She knew there were no really dangerous animals left in the jungles around the ruins.

She went down the steps, her eyes on the bushes where she had heard the sound. Then she caught a glimpse of a small, hairy form, and two bright eyes peered out of the bushes at her. She almost laughed in her relief. Now she recognized it—the little pug dog from Cottage 3. Surely it shouldn't be wandering out here at night—something might happen to it. It must have gotten out somehow. Perhaps she should catch it and take it back.

She stepped out onto the walk and whistled softly. "Here, fellow," she called persuasively. "Come on now." She held out her hand as though she had something to give the animal. The dog stared at her but didn't move. The moon was bright and she could see it distinctly. She walked slowly toward it.

There was a slight sound on the walk behind her, but before she could turn to see what it was, something smooth and slippery covered her face and she couldn't breathe. She tried to struggle, but something was holding her. Darkness descended. . . .

CHAPTER THREE

When Lori opened her eyes, Brian was there, his arm under her head. He was looking down at her with an expression of alarm.

"Lori, what happened?" he cried.

She clutched him in terror. "Oh, Brian! Something attacked me—it pulled something over my head so I couldn't breathe—"

"But what were you doing out here?"

"I heard something moving around, like an animal of some sort. I came out to see what it was—it was that little pug dog—and while I was trying to coax it out of the bushes, somebody came up behind me and pulled what felt like a plastic bag over my head. I struggled, but I couldn't get it off—

then I guess I passed out. How did you find me so quickly? I didn't have time to yell—"

"Let me get you inside," he said, "then we'll talk about it." He lifted her to her feet, and she clung to him, still feeling rather wobbly.

He helped her into the cottage and settled her on the bed, then sat down next to her, holding her hand.

"I heard that dog barking," he explained. "I knew that it gets out of the cottage sometimes and wanders around, so I thought I'd better take it home. When I came out, the dog was gone, but you were lying there on the walk."

"Wasn't there anything over my head?"

"Not a thing. Maybe I'd better go out now and take a look around."

"Maybe you should," she agreed.

He went out but was back a short time later. "I can't find a trace of anything," he told her. "Even the dog seems to have gone home. Tell me again just what happened."

She sighed and pushed back her long, silky hair. "There really isn't much to tell. As I said, I went outside to see what was prowling around the cottage and saw the pug in the bushes. I called it, but it wouldn't come. I was just standing there on the walk when someone came up behind me and pulled something over my head. I suppose you think this is more hysterical imaginings, like the face at the window," she added bitterly.

"No, of course not. But it looks as though someone is trying to frighten you rather than do you any real harm. I mean—if someone had wanted to kill you, all he'd have to do would be to hold the bag in place a few more minutes. Instead—"

"I know, Brian," she said with a shiver. "You don't have to spell it out."

"But there has to be some reason for these frightening tricks, Lori. You just got here. Nobody knows you—it doesn't make any sense. Unless you know of some reason—" He looked at her searchingly. "Have you been followed here by someone? A rejected boyfriend maybe?"

She smiled in spite of her distress. "No, nothing like that. If there *is* someone trying to frighten me away, it has to be connected with what happened here twelve years ago."

"Do you want to tell me about it?"

"I suppose I'd better, since you seem to be getting involved anyway. I think I was witness to a murder, but nobody believed me at the time. If it were true, and the murderer is still around, I can see why he might want to get rid of me—before I start poking around, trying to remember what I really did see."

Brian looked startled. "A murder? But that could be very bad for you—very dangerous. Suppose you tell me what you can remember of it."

"You already know that I was here with my father when he was working on the restoration. He had hired a few college students to do fieldwork for extra credit. I developed a terrific crush on one of them. His name was Erik Holstrom. He was of Swedish descent, and they called him the Viking because he was so big and blond. Of course he didn't pay any attention to me. I was just a skinny kid. My father didn't think much of him—said he wasn't dedicated enough to the work and would never make a good archaeologist.

"I was always doing a lot of exploring around the ruins, sometimes wandering off on my own into the unrestored sections, which was strictly forbidden. Erik and another of the students were in the cottage next door, the one you're in now. The furniture was arranged differently then, and my cot was up against the window where the big bed is now. Daddy had them put up a screen so I'd have some privacy. He was always dead tired at night and would go right to sleep. Sometimes I'd sneak out at night and go over to the ruins—"

"That sounds really dangerous. Weren't you afraid? I don't think I'd want to hang around over there at night."

"It was spooky all right, but I loved it. I was always hoping I'd see some ghosts of past sacrificial victims or something, but I never did. Anyway, on this particular night, I was lying on my cot wondering if I should go to the ruins or get some sleep for a change, when I heard a low whistle next door. I got up on my knees to look out the window, and I saw Erik come out. He went around the cottage, and I saw another man step out of the shadows and join him. I couldn't see who it was. They disappeared around the back of the cottage."

"You're sure it was a man and not a woman?"

"Oh, yes. He was tall and thin, and I could tell by his walk that it was a man. I was curious to see what they were up to, so I pulled out the screen—I was getting very good at that—and climbed out the window."

"In your pajamas?"

"Sure, there wasn't time to dress. I ran around the cottage just in time to see them going through a gate back there that opens onto a path into the jungle."

"It's still there."

"Have you explored to see where the path leads?" she asked eagerly.

"No, but I've always intended to. Julian said it goes to an abandoned village back in the jungle."

"Oh. I don't know anything about that. There are other paths branching off. I was too curious to turn back, so I followed the men into the jungle. I had a little trouble keeping up, and I was afraid a jaguar or something might get me, but I kept going.

"We must have walked about half a mile, and I was about ready to give up and turn back because I'd lost sight of the men. Then I came out into a clearing. In the middle of it was an unrestored pyramid. Not a big one, maybe thirty feet high or so. Of course it was nearly covered by vegetation, but there was a path cleared up the side to the top platform. The men were standing up there. The moon was bright, so I could see quite clearly, but I never did see the face of the second man. I stopped at the edge of the clearing and watched them.

"The other man seemed to be doing something, I couldn't see what. Then, suddenly, a stone seemed to move. I guess it uncovered the entrance to the pyramid, because they went inside and disappeared."

"I suppose you followed them?"

"Not immediately. I knew Erik would be furious if he found out I'd followed them to the pyramid. I'd just about decided to turn back and go home, but then my curiosity got the better of me. I climbed up the pyramid and peered in. There was a bend in the stone stairs, so I couldn't see all the way to the bottom. But I could see a light flickering down there. I was trying to decide whether to go any farther when I heard a terrible cry. I can't describe it, it was like nothing I'd heard before, but somehow I knew it was a death cry." She stopped with a shudder at the memory of that awful sound.

"For heaven's sake, Lori, go on! What did you do then?"

"I had to find out what was happening—it had sounded like Erik's voice. So I stumbled down the stairs to the bend, where I could see the rest of the way. I stopped—and all I can remember now is seeing a dim form standing there with its back to me, holding a knife covered with blood—and Erik on the floor with blood gushing out of his chest. There was a lantern beside him, and something else, something that gleamed and seemed to have the face of the feathered serpent on it. I started to go to him, but I tripped and fell and must have hit my head on the stairs, because that's all I can remember."

"That's all? But where were you when you regained consciousness?"

"Wandering on the road the next morning, mumbling something about a feathered serpent."

"You mean you don't know how you got out of the pyramid, or what happened to the people in it?"

"I only know that Erik was dead."

"Was the one with the knife the same person who accompanied him into the pyramid?"

"I'm not sure. It was so murky down there, and I was really looking only at Erik. It all happened so fast. I have no idea how I got out of there—that's one of the gaps in my memory, and one reason I came back here. I thought that seeing this place again would bring everything back. But so far it hasn't."

"Probably one of the people—either the man who accompanied Erik to the pyramid, or his murderer—carried you out and left you on the road."

She shuddered. "No, Brian, I don't think so. While I don't remember what happened between the time I fell down the stairs and was found on the road, I think part of it comes back in a nightmare I've been having off and on since that time."

"What sort of nightmare?" He leaned over and gently stroked her disheveled hair.

"I—I don't like to talk about it. But I wake up and find myself in the dark down in the pyramid, and I know there's a bloody body beside me and I scream. It varies, but that's about it."

"But it doesn't explain how you got out?"

"No."

"Well, anyway, what happened after they found you on the road?"

"They took me to a hospital in Mérida. I was there a couple of days. Because I kept insisting Erik had been murdered, the police had me take them into the jungle to find the pyramid, but I couldn't find the right path. The one I thought was it just led to some more ruins, some sort of building with nothing in it. Mother had come down by then to take me home. They decided it had been just a nightmare."

"But Erik was gone?"

"Yes, but he'd left a note in his cottage saying he was going away—to South America—and wasn't coming back. His car was gone and so were all his clothes. The car was later found abandoned in Cancun, and since a yacht owned by some man that Erik knew had sailed that morning, they assumed he was on it. They never bothered to check up, because nobody was interested. Nobody but me. Mother took me home, and that was the end of it."

"Didn't Erik have a family?"

"Only an old aunt who was putting him through college. She said she'd expected him to do something like that, that he was always unstable. Her husband had been a colleague of Daddy's, and that's why he gave Erik a job. The aunt had insisted that Erik become an archaeologist like her husband, but he'd never really cared for it."

"Did anybody know what Erik was up to?"

"His roommate said he thought Erik had found some artifact that he was going to sell to this multi-millionaire collector on the yacht. He also said that Erik had drugged him that night to keep him out of the way."

"Are you sure Erik was really dead? Maybe he killed the other man and then ran away to South America on the yacht to live on the money he got from the artifact."

"No, it was Erik. I saw him lying there, all bloody—"

"All right, forget that part. It could have been the other man, his partner, who took his belongings and car and ran away because he didn't want to share the money. And maybe he's the one trying to scare you away now. But why would he come back here now? That doesn't make sense."

"I know. Still, there must be a reason. Maybe he's afraid my memory will come back and I'll remember who he was. I don't think I would, though. I don't think I ever saw who else was in the pyramid with Erik."

"It might have been one of the other students— or some native who showed him where to find the artifact."

"There are many possibilities. But I didn't come here to play detective. I'd just like to find the pyramid and prove that it wasn't a nightmare. If his body is still there, let the police worry about that."

"It seems an odd coincidence, though, that he'd show up here the same time as you after twelve years."

"I know. But there might be a reason—unless, of course, it was someone who's been here all along."

"What reason could there be?"

"Maybe the same thing that started me thinking about coming back here. There was a little item in the newspaper about some American foundation that was going to send a group down here next fall to restore another section of the city. I'm pretty sure that section will include the area behind the hotel where the pyramid was. That would mean they would probably clean it up and open it—and find Erik's body."

"I see. Yes, that might bring the murderer here, but then why hasn't he moved the remains and left? Why would he be hanging around?"

"I don't know. Maybe he can't find the pyramid

after all these years. I couldn't even find it again at the time."

"You say it was the article that brought you down?"

"It started me thinking about it. I'd always had it in the back of my mind to come here again, and I was free this summer. I realized when I saw the article that if I waited any longer, I might not be free to search the jungle alone."

"Is that what you intend to do? I don't think that's a good idea, in view of what's been happening. At least let me go with you."

"But you have your own work to do," she objected.

"I'm practically through now. And what could be more important than protecting you?"

"That's very gallant of you." She sighed and sat up. "It's terribly late, Brian. You'd better go now. We'll talk more in the morning."

"Well, don't go outside—no matter *what* you hear. Yell for me." He moved slowly toward the door. "Let me know when you want to go over for breakfast."

He went out, and she got up and locked the door to the porch. Then, totally exhausted, she crawled into bed, turned out the light, and fell into a troubled sleep.

She awoke around eight feeling rested. She sang cheerfully in the tepid shower, then put on shorts and a T-shirt and braided her long hair into one thick plait. In spite of the awful thing that had happened here all those years ago, this cottage still held some very fond memories for her. She reflected that the happiest times of her life had been when she was allowed to grub around in the dirt at some dig with her father. If he had lived, she would doubtless have become an archaeologist. Well, she wouldn't go off into the jungle today. She'd simply see the sights like any tourist.

When she was ready, she went over to Brian's cottage and rapped on his screen door. He came to the door with a welcoming smile, dressed in shorts and a sport shirt.

"Good morning, princess! Everything okay? No more 'ghoulies and ghosties, long-leggety beasties, and things that go bump in the night'?"

"Not a thing," she assured him. "I slept like a log or a top or whatever it is that's such a great sleeper, and now I'm starved and I need some coffee. I sure wished I'd had some of my own this morning."

"We'll get you some right after breakfast," he promised.

Breakfast was served buffet style on the terrace overlooking the pond. There was a lot of fresh fruit —pineapple, sliced avocado, melon—as well as several kinds of juice. There were scrambled eggs, bacon, and pans of things she couldn't identify, also the inevitable black beans. There were baskets of rolls and bread—slighty toasted but cold—and butter and jelly.

Lori took pineapple, a small helping of eggs, two slices of bacon, and a toasted bun. Brian loaded his plate with everything in sight. Finally they found a table near the railing. A waiter was going around to the tables, filling the cups with coffee or tea.

The garden was lovely in the morning with the sun shining on all the exotic blooms and the glittering fountain. Even the Chac-Mool looked a bit less forbidding, although his vacant, uncaring gaze still unnerved her.

"That thing is enough to take away my appetite," she murmured.

"Some authorities claim he's holding a solar disk in his bowl, so he may not be as bad as you think. The experts disagree on everything concerning the Mayans. Some say they weren't bloodthirsty until the Toltecs came along and introduced them to their nasty little ways. Others claim the Mayans always had some form of human sacrifice."

"I'm sure they did," Lori said. "I know that Chac-Mool was used for something evil—I can feel it."

While they ate, she kept glancing around the terrace, but none of the other cottage people showed up. Probably they all fixed their own breakfasts in their cottages, which was a sensible idea. When she and Brian had finished eating, they went to Brian's car and drove out along the highway to a little grocery store, where she purchased instant coffee, milk, cornflakes, and some sweet rolls. Brian spotted a bottle of Kahlúa at an amazingly low price, so he bought that. He said that if Lori were to go on at the rate she had started, they might need a spot of something in their coffee at night to settle their nerves.

After they had taken the supplies back to the hotel, they gathered up what they needed for a jaunt to the ruins and started out. The rainy season hadn't started yet, but although it was only the end of March, the heat was making itself felt. When they got to the hotel's main entrance, a tour bus was there to pick up a group that was leaving. People were coming out of the hotel loaded with flight bags and extra shopping bags of goodies they'd bought and couldn't pack, and everyone was standing around talking and laughing. Julian was there, standing beside the tour leader, supervising the transfer of luggage, but he came over when he saw Brian and Lori.

"Are you going over to the ruins?" he asked politely.

"Yes. I want to revive some old memories," she told him.

He gave her a quick, rather tense glance, then gestured toward the crowd of people. "This group is going on to Uxmal today," he said. "The tours are nearly over now for the season, but of course we will still have individual guests like you. Have a good morning." He went back to help with the loading.

Brian and Lori headed for the ruins. The main entrance was about a quarter of a mile up the road.

"I read up on Chichén Itzá before I came here," Brian told her, "but since your father was an archaeologist, you probably know more about it than I do."

"Oh, I've forgotten most of what I learned back then," she admitted, "except that Chichén Itzá was founded around 432 A.D. and that it's the largest and best restored of the temple cities."

"But there's still a lot of it left unrestored in the jungle."

"Yes, it extends for miles around here. Oh, look, we can see the big pyramid from here—" She pointed off to their left where they could see the flat top of it extending above the trees. "Tell me about that serpent ceremony, Brian. I wish I'd gotten here in time for that."

"Maybe it's just as well you didn't. It attracts all the kooks and crazy cults from all over. It's much quieter here now. Anyway, as you know, they built the pyramid so that at the exact time of the spring equinox the shadow cast along the edge seems to undulate like a giant snake. I got some good shots of it."

They walked on in the bright sunlight, their eyes on the great mass of the distant pyramid.

"Where do you want to go first?" Brian asked.

"The sacred spring, I believe," she told him.

The road to the *cenote* ran straight from the Temple of Kukulcan. It wasn't much more than a lane, bordered by trees. It was very peaceful and quiet, except for the inevitable chattering tourists. As she walked, Lori thought about Julian's dream.

When she and Brian reached the *cenote,* she could hear one of the guides making the usual speech about how whenever things went wrong, such as a bad drought that ruined the crops, they'd throw people into the pool: prisoners, slaves, children, people of all ages.

Lori and Brian climbed higher on the rocks to get a better view. It was a large, roughly round pool that looked like an abandoned stone quarry. High walls of rock extended above the water, perhaps sixty feet below where they stood. Lori could see a number of what looked like small caves in the face of the cliff, with large lizards running in and out.

Caves. Something stirred in the back of her mind. *Something about a cave—* Then the impression was gone. The water looked muddy and unattractive, with a green scum over parts of it.

"How deep is it?" someone asked the guide.

"About forty feet. There's a lot of sludge in the bottom."

Lori got out her camera and climbed higher until she found a flat rock directly overlooking the spring. She was trying to visualize the sacrificial rites, but it wasn't easy with all the tourists milling around. Here there was no railing, but a little farther up there was a stone platform with a stone balustrade at the edge; perhaps that was where the victims were thrown from.

The crowd was so dense up there that she decided to stay where she was and take her pictures from there. As she was sighting through the viewfinder, a new tour group came up behind her, and suddenly someone let out a shout: "Look! It's a quetzal!"

She looked up in amazement as a large bird flew right over her head and on out across the pool. It was an incredibly beautiful creature with bronze-green and red plumage and two long, flowing plumes on its tail.

The guide said in an awed voice: "I can't believe it! The sacred quetzal bird, and they don't even breed in this part of the country! It's like a sign from the gods—"

The bird veered back, and as the crowd surged forward, cameras clicking wildly, Lori felt a sharp shove against her back, and then she was on the ground, halfway over the edge and sliding rapidly!

CHAPTER FOUR

It happened so quickly Lori didn't have time to think. One minute she was standing on the ledge; the next she was halfway over it. She was hanging on to the rock with a frantic grip, but she could feel her hands slipping. Then she felt her arm grabbed, and strong arms pulled her back to safety. It was the tour guide from the group that had come up behind her, and he was babbling excitedly:

"Oh, señorita! You were going into the *cenote!* Someone must have jostled you!"

The other tourists crowded around, all talking at once in loud voices.

"The bird—we were looking at the bird, and—"

"—and I told Sam, 'Sam,' I said, 'that girl had better be careful'—"

Then Brian was there, clutching her frantically. "Lori, Lori! What happened?"

Except for a scraped knee where she had hit the ledge, she seemed none the worse for her experience.

"Thank you, thank you very much," she said to the tour guide.

"But, Lori," Brian persisted, "how did it happen? I was trying to get a shot of the quetzal, so I wasn't looking. Then I heard people yelling, and there you were—going over the edge! I couldn't reach you in time—"

She looked at the people around her, at their excited, curious, and sympathetic faces, and she couldn't say "Somebody pushed me!" So she simply said, "Everybody was running to see the bird, and I suppose someone knocked against me. I know I was too near the edge. Did anyone actually see what happened?"

They all looked blank. "We were too busy watching the bird," one woman finally said. "A quetzal, you know. Very rare."

"Indeed," the guide said. "They breed in the highlands of Guatemala. In the past only the nobles and priests could wear their feathers. You were very lucky to see one. As I said, it was like a sign from the gods."

Lori made a wry face. "Sure—from old Quet-zalcoatl himself—he very nearly got himself an-other sacrifice!"

Brian pulled at her arm. "Come on, Lori. Let's get away from here."

She thanked the guide again, and they walked away. Brian looked down at her searchingly. "Was that all there was to it?" he asked. "You got jostled in the surge to see the bird?"

She shrugged. "I don't know. It felt like someone pushed me, but it could have been an accident. You know how everybody crowded up to get a shot of the bird. And I *was* awfully near the edge."

"Maybe. But I don't like the way things keep happening to you."

"I'm not exactly ecstatic about it myself."

"You got a good look at the people around you, didn't you? Did anyone look even vaguely familiar? I mean—could there have been someone from the past—"

"They just looked like tourists to me." Was he suggesting that Erik's murderer might have been there behind her? A frightening thought. But they had all been strangers. Except—Brian himself. He had been very close. She had only his word for it that he had been busy photographing the bird. It occurred to her that Brian was exactly the right age to have been one of the other students. She really couldn't remember what any of the others had looked like; she barely remembered what Erik looked like. And since she'd come back to Mexico, Brian had been there every time something happened to her. She didn't want to suspect him. But she didn't dare not to.

"He could have slipped away in the crowd," Brian said. Then he noticed that she was limping. "You're hurt, Lori. Let me see."

They stopped, and he examined her knee. "It's badly scraped; it needs to be treated."

"I have a first-aid kit in my suitcase. I'll take care of it when I get back to my cottage. Really, Brian, it's nothing. You should have seen me when I was here before—always covered with scrapes and bruises from climbing around the ruins."

Later, when they got back to the cottage, she washed, disinfected, and put a bandage on her knee. Then, when she had tidied herself up a bit, they went over to the hotel for lunch.

"I don't suppose you feel like doing any more exploring today," he said when they had finished.

"Not particularly," she admitted. "My knee is a bit stiff. I think I'll just take it easy by the pool. I won't go in the water, though, because of my knee."

"If you're sure you'll be all right, I'll go back to the ruins for a while. There are some more shots I want to get."

"Of course I'll be all right. What could happen by the pool?"

"Who knows? With your luck, the Creature from

the Black Lagoon is likely to rise out of it and drag you down into the depths!"

"I'll take my chances," she said, smiling at him. How could she possibly suspect Brian? And yet—

"You know, Lori," he said, "I was just thinking —I was taking pictures almost continuously while the bird was flying over, hoping to get at least one good shot of it. It's possible that one of them might show something that was going on around you, at least who was standing directly behind you."

She felt a wave of hope. If that were true, it would exonerate Brian—provided the pictures showed that he was not very close at that moment.

"That's a good idea. Can you develop them right away?"

"Unfortunately, I don't have the equipment to do my own developing. As I said, we usually buy free-lance material. I just know enough to take reasonably good pictures when I'm on a story myself. Then I take the negatives home for an expert to work on."

"I doubt if there's anyplace around here that could do it. You'll probably have to take the negatives to Mérida."

"I'll talk to Julian about it and see what he suggests. Fortunately I have only a few shots left in that roll. I'll finish it this afternoon."

"All right. You go on and do your work while I loll around the pool."

Brian went off to the ruins, and Lori put on her

bathing suit and went over to the lovely little pool. It was a hot afternoon, and there were quite a few other people there, some swimming, some sunning themselves, and others sitting at the little tables sipping drinks.

She spread her beach towel on the tiles near the water and lay down, after liberally dousing herself with suntan lotion. She knew from bitter experience in the Caribbean how searing the tropical sun could be, and she had been back in Chicago long enough to lose some of her protective tan.

The sun felt good, and she was just about to doze off when a shadow fell across her body and a voice said:

"Miss Cahill?"

She opened her eyes and looked up into the dark gaze of the beautiful young man she'd noticed the night before. He was gazing down at her with the same intent expression she had observed then.

"Yes?" she replied. Seen close up he was even better-looking than she had thought. He was wearing white bathing trunks that showed off a nice, compact body, beautifully tanned and just muscular enough to be attractive. His cap of bronze curls gleamed in the sunlight, and his smile revealed even white teeth.

"I'm Max Forrest from Cottage One," he said. "Julian told me who you were. I wonder if you'd mind if I sketched you?"

It was an offer no red-blooded woman could

refuse. She smiled up at him. "Why not? So long as I don't have to pose in any uncomfortable position."

"You don't even have to move. You're fine just the way you are."

She was lying on her back, arms folded under her head, one knee bent, the other—the wounded one—stretched straight out.

"I thought you were here to sketch ruins," she said.

He laughed. "And you would hardly qualify there, would you?" He sat down nearby, sketch pad on his knee. "Yes, that's why I'm here. I've been commissioned to do a portfolio of Chichén Itzá sketches for a book, but that doesn't mean I can't do something on my own when I see something good."

He started making rapid lines on the paper. "I'll leave out the bandage, of course. I understand you had a mishap over at the *cenote* this morning."

News certainly got around fast! "How did you know that?" she asked.

"I heard some tourists talking, and Julian told me it was you. You must have had quite a scare."

"It was a bit unnerving," she admitted, giving him a thoughtful glance. Could Max have been a student here once? Could he have been behind her at the sacred spring? But surely she or Brian would have seen him! She hoped Brian could get those pictures developed soon. She hated having to suspect everyone around her.

"I understand you're a musician," he said as he continued sketching.

Julian again, she supposed. They must have had quite a little chat about her! But why had Max been so interested? Was it because of her irresistible charm—or was there a more sinister reason?

She told him something about her career, without mentioning the fact that she had been at Chichén Itzá before. Then she asked him about himself, but he seemed curiously reluctant to tell her anything beyond a few bare facts. She found out that he lived in San Diego and that he had been an art student and part-time actor—mainly in television commercials—before he got his present position as illustrator for a well-known writer of books about ancient ruins. The writer's name—when Lori pressed him for more details—was Jane Barnard.

"Is she an archaeologist?" Lori asked.

"No, but she's made it her hobby. She writes books that a layman can understand, and they're quite popular."

"I should think she'd use photographs," Lori said.

Max shrugged. Something glinted in his dark eyes for a moment and then was gone. "She did in the beginning, but then she saw some of my work and decided that drawings might be more effective. It's worked out quite well."

"Doesn't she usually come with you when you go on location?"

"Oh, yes, but a few weeks ago she fell and broke her leg. So she sent me on alone. She has all the material she needs anyway."

"How old is she?" Lori asked idly, but with considerable interest.

He shrugged again and his gaze slid away. "I'm not sure. Around fifty, I guess."

When Lori asked him where he had spent his childhood, he grew very vague and muttered something about the Midwest. Not a word about a family. Lori gave up and closed her eyes, trying to relax in the sunlight.

She had just about dozed off when he announced that he had finished. She sat up to look at his sketch. Somehow he had made her look very seductive, and he had certainly given her more curves than she actually possessed. The bathing suit was a bit skimpier than the one she was wearing too. He made her look sexy, and he hadn't caught the real essence of her at all, which was an elusive something in between gamine and enchanted princess — or so she had been told by others.

He saw that she was frowning, and he said, "You don't like it."

"It's well done," she replied, "but it makes me look like something I'm not."

"That's the way I see you," he said, looking a bit sulky.

She didn't believe him. She knew she didn't project that kind of sex appeal.

"Maybe I should try again with the ruins for a background," he suggested. "Would you like that better?"

She wondered if Julian had told him about her previous visit. But she didn't intend to mention it if he didn't. "Perhaps I would," she agreed.

He rose, tucking the pad under his arm. "I'd better get back to my real job. I wonder if you'd like to have dinner with me tonight, Lori? We could go to one of the other hotels—perhaps the Mayaland. It's quite famous, lots of royalty and presidents and movie stars have stayed there."

She thought about it. Perhaps it would be a good idea to find out more about him. After all, that was why she was here—to follow up any possibility of learning the truth about Erik. "All right, Max," she agreed. But she wasn't really thrilled by the prospect. For some reason she felt a bit uncomfortable with him.

He left, and she turned over onto her stomach to give the other side an equal opportunity for burning. Later she returned to her cottage, took a cold shower, and lay down for a nap. Finally, around six, she was awakened by a tapping on her screen door, which she had cautiously latched. She got up groggily and went to look out. It was Brian, freshly showered and dressed in a nice summer suit.

"Hi," he said cheerfully. "I thought you'd like to

know that I asked Julian about developing film, and he said that although there isn't any shop around here, he thinks there's a guy over at the Mayaland who was taking pictures for some important magazine and was doing his own developing. He suggested that I talk to him, so I went over, and he offered to do the roll for me. Said he'd have them in the morning."

"That's great," she said. "Did you tell him why you wanted them?"

"Not the whole story, of course. I said I thought I'd gotten some good shots of the quetzal. He was quite excited about that, because he hadn't been there. And when I offered to give him one if they turned out well, he was eager to develop them for me. So it wasn't merely an altruistic gesture. By the way, I thought you might enjoy having dinner over there tonight."

She stared at him blankly. "Oh, Brian, I'm sorry. I've already accepted an invitation to have dinner there."

His happy smile faded. He looked like a little boy, told she couldn't come out and play. "You do? Who with? Or shouldn't I ask?"

"You may ask. Max Forrest, the artist in Cottage One. He was sketching me by the pool."

"I don't dare turn my back on you for a minute! I suppose I've been taking too much for granted too quickly."

"Maybe you have," she agreed. "We aren't exactly going steady, you know." She couldn't help feeling a bit ashamed, although there was no reason she shouldn't go out with someone else. She knew that if Brian had asked another girl to dinner at the Mayaland, she'd have been furious. And he looked so nice, all dressed up in his suit. . . .

"Will I see you tomorrow?" he asked sadly.

"Why not? I'll be around."

"I hope so," he said darkly. "But be careful. After all, you don't know anything about this guy."

"I know. He's just a pickup—like you."

Brian winced. "All right, I'll go quietly. I'll bring the pictures over to show you as soon as I get them in the morning. *Ciao,* my love." He ambled off toward the dining room to eat his lonely meal.

Lori didn't know how formal they were at the Mayaland, but just to be on the safe side, she put on the one formal gown she'd brought along: a simple white lace affair with a wide blue satin sash.

She was glad she'd worn it when Max arrived looking resplendent in a light beige tropical suit with a pale yellow shirt and brown silk tie, his curls gleaming like melted gold under the porch light. Repressing an urge to give vent to a wolf whistle, Lori merely smiled and said, "Hi, Max."

"You look lovely, Lori," he told her. "Like a girl going to her first prom. I see now that you were right—I didn't paint you properly."

* * *

It turned out to be a pleasant evening, but to Lori it somehow seemed a bit strange. From the beginning she had the feeling that they were two actors, made up for their parts and rather good at them. Her first sight of the Mayaland Hotel did not impress her. On the edge of the ruins, it was a four-story, ocher-colored building, rather shabby and crumbling-looking like her own hotel. Apparently they got that way very quickly in this climate.

But once they had entered through the elaborate wrought-iron gates, she began to see why the Mayaland was so famous. It was like the exotic set of some old movie, with its high ceilings, beautiful tiled floors, and heavy, old-fashioned furniture. There was no air-conditioning, only ceiling fans, with many balconies and open walkways between rooms. The jungle was very near. All the staff seemed to be dressed in white.

They had drinks on the main veranda, then went into the dining room for dinner, where they were serenaded from a second-floor balcony. Lori was a bit startled by a strange, rather gruesome mural, which portrayed Mayan gods, Christ, and an odd assortment of severed heads.

"It doesn't do much for my appetite," she commented.

There was one rather curious incident during the meal. About halfway through it she began to have the feeling that she was being watched. It was much the same feeling she'd had the first night when Max had been staring at her so intently, but it couldn't be Max this time. She looked carefully around the room, wondering if Brian had followed them there to keep an eye on her. There was no sign of him, but over near the arched entrance of the dining room she saw a man, possibly in his late thirties or early forties, neatly dressed in a plain black suit.

Sometimes she liked to watch old movies on TV, and there was one actor, George Raft, who usually played the part of a gangster. This man looked a lot like him: same slight figure, dark eyes, and patent-leather hair. She remembered one movie in particular in which Raft was always standing around tossing a coin. For some reason there was something rather sinister about the way he kept tossing it.

This man wasn't tossing a coin, but somehow he gave the impression that he was. He was staring intently in their direction, and for a fleeting moment his eyes met hers. Then he slipped quietly out of the room. Lori felt a faint tremor of alarm. She glanced at Max, but apparently he hadn't noticed the man.

Later they danced, and Lori realized that all the women in the room were staring at Max and probably drooling. He danced smoothly, gracefully, with beautiful muscular coordination, and seemed to exude a sort of aura of male sexuality. Lori supposed she ought to feel thrilled, but somehow all she could feel was a total sense of unreality. Once she thought she glimpsed the Raft character watching them again from a distance, but she wasn't sure.

At the door of her cottage she turned to face Max. This was it, the Moment of Truth. It was how a man behaved at this point in their relationship that gave him his final grade, scoring from one to ten. There were so many fine points of gradation between perfection and utter jerkdom.

He took her hands and stood looking down at her. The fountain was splashing in the background, and a nearly full moon rode high above the jungle trees. She looked into his dark eyes and saw the light of desire glowing there. But then, as she gazed into them, something came into his eyes, replacing the glow—and it was as though a glass wall had dropped between them. He dropped her hands as though they had burned him, and murmured, "Good night, Lori." Then he strode off toward his own cottage, leaving her standing there in astonishment and some chagrin.

Well, my girl, she thought, *so much for your devastating charm!* She went into the cottage and stared into the mirror over the little dresser. She couldn't see anything that might frighten a man off. She had let her hair hang loose that evening; it was a bit windblown now, and there was a slight flush in her cheeks. What had happened? Well, it was a puzzlement, as the King of Siam would say. She made a face at herself and went to bed.

She was tired enough to fall asleep quickly in spite of her confusing thoughts, and she slept soundly for several hours. But then the nightmare came. She had not had it for quite a long time now, but she had been expecting it here in its place of origin.

It was always the same. She was in a totally dark place smelling of age and death, vaguely aware of stone walls closing her in. She was aware of terror —blind, unreasoning terror—and she knew that somewhere not very far from where she lay was a dead thing, a thing of horror, covered with blood. She tried to move, to crawl away, fearful that the dead thing would move toward her, and she knew that if it touched her she would die from sheer horror—

CHAPTER FIVE

Lori awoke as she always did, moaning and gasping and drenched in sweat. Now she became aware of a banging on the door, a voice demanding to be let in. She switched on her light and, still half asleep and weak with horror, staggered across the room and unlocked the door. She didn't care who was there—she just wanted some human contact. Brian rushed in, seized her in his arms, and looked wildly around the room for her unknown assailant.

"Where did he go?" he cried.

"No, Brian," she managed to say, "no one was here. It was just my nightmare." She sagged against him and he picked her up and carried her back to her bed.

"I must say, nights are more interesting since you got here," he remarked.

"Did I make a frightful din?" she asked.

"Not really. The window by my bed is just opposite yours, and I was awake anyway. It sounded as though someone was attacking you, and I thought maybe Forrest—"

"Brian! He wasn't here. He didn't even come in."

"I know. I heard him bring you home and then leave. But I thought he might have come back later—"

"Well, he didn't. And anyway, what business was it of yours to stay awake waiting for me to come home? You're acting like a father."

"I assure you that I couldn't feel less fatherly than I do at this moment. And I can't help it if you give me insomnia."

She pulled away from him. "Thank you for coming, Brian, but I think you'd better go now. I'll be all right."

He stood up reluctantly. "This nightmare—" he began. "I wish you'd describe it in more detail."

"It's just that I wake up and find myself in a dark, enclosed space—the pyramid—with what I know is a dead body beside me. And I know I have to—to get away before it touches me—" She put her hands over her face and added in a muffled voice, "It's the horror I feel that makes it so awful. Not really anything that happens."

He put a comforting hand on her shoulder. "And you think that it really happened to you?"

"Yes, I'm sure of it, only I can't remember what I did after that—how I got out of the pyramid."

"And so you've come back to try to find out—and somebody here doesn't seem to want you to," he said thoughtfully.

"That's about it. But I'm not leaving, Brian. Not until I find that pyramid."

"Okay, but promise me you won't go off into the jungle alone. Let me go with you."

"All right," she said, but even as she promised, she was wondering if it would be wise to go off into the jungle with him. How could she trust anyone?

She slept late the next morning and was too late for the hotel buffet, so she made coffee and ate a roll. She was just finishing when Brian came to the door. When she let him in, he waved a manila envelope at her.

"I've got them!" he announced triumphantly.

"The pictures? Oh, Brian! How did they turn out?"

"I got some dandy ones of the bird. The fellow who developed them for me was ecstatic."

"But do they reveal anything about who might have pushed me?" she asked impatiently.

"See for yourself." He spread them out on the table, and she leaned over them anxiously.

He was right about the bird: There was one particularly good one of the bird shown against the blue sky. Then there were some jumbled ones showing the crowd surrounding her on the ledge. None of the faces showed very clearly, because, of course, everyone had his back to the camera. A few faces were in partial profile.

She saw herself, camera to her eye, snapping the bird as it flew over her head. The closest people to her seemed to be a short, rather stout lady with flaming red hair and a tall, thin man. The man seemed to be looking at her, and part of his profile was revealed. Lori pointed to him.

"I think I've seen that man before!" she exclaimed. "He was on the terrace with Max."

"Yes, that's Dr. Parker, the retired archaeologist in Cottage Four."

"But he didn't stay around after I fell. Did you see him there?"

"I was too concerned about you to notice much of anything."

"I've got to talk to him, Brian. Find out if he was here when my father was."

"You could ask Julian—he would probably know."

She was relieved that at least the pictures didn't show Max anywhere around, and Brian couldn't have been too close if he had been busy taking pictures. But then she realized that none of these pictures had been taken at the moment she was

pushed. Brian could have moved closer, or someone else could have appeared.

"I'm afraid they don't tell us much after all," she
said, turning away. "But I will try to find out more
about Dr. Parker. What are you going to do this
morning, Brian?"

"I thought I'd go over and take some shots of the
Observatory. I'm not too satisfied with the ones
I've got. Or were you planning on an expedition
into the jungle?"

"No, that can wait another day. My knee's stiff
this morning, and I don't feel like walking for any
distance. I'll tag along with you."

"Good. I don't like to let you out of my sight."

Lori picked up the canvas bag she always carried
and followed him out. The Observatory, he told
her, was over in the so-called old section of the
city; the new section contained the area of the great
pyramid, sometimes called the Castle, and was surrounded by other buildings in what seemed to form
a vast square.

They approached the Observatory, stopping some
distance off for Brian to take a shot of it. Lori
thought it quite impressive, with its dome silhou-
etted against the pure blue of the sky. It did look
very much like a modern observatory, except that it
contained no telescope and the dome couldn't be
opened.

"Have you ever been up in it?" Brian asked.

"Once with my father. There's a spiral staircase

that winds all the way up into the observation chamber at the top, but it's hard climbing. I remember that there were openings along the way that Daddy explained fixed astronomically important lines of sight."

"They were very clever, those Mayans."

They went on, and Lori said, "I think I'll wander around a bit on my own while you take your pictures. I'll come back here in a little while."

He looked a bit dubious. "All right, but no wandering off into the jungle. Stay where there are other people."

She walked away, knowing where she wanted to go. She knew that from here the other spring—the one called the Xtoloc Well—was nearby.

The old part of the temple city was surrounded by the scrubby jungle, and soon she reached the edge of it. She knew there was a path there somewhere that led to the well, and after a few minutes she found it—not a road like the one to the Well of Sacrifice, but a good enough path. As she walked along it, something kept tugging at her memory. She knew she had been there with her father. They'd even climbed down the cliff, where there was a path of sorts, to look at the caves. There were lots of caves around in the cliff, but there was one that was bigger and seemed to go far back. They hadn't entered it, but there was something he had said— She concentrated, trying to remember.

They were natural caves, he had said, but it was

possible the Mayans had dug the big one deeper and used it for something. Oh, yes—he'd said it wouldn't surprise him if it connected with a temple somewhere, another route the priests could take with their mysterious comings and goings. They liked to pop out unexpectedly and surprise the worshipers. Tricks to all trades, he'd said.

She'd wanted to go in and explore, but he'd said no, it would be dangerous to go into it, since the caves hadn't been used for a long time and might collapse. He'd warned her to stay away from there when she was out exploring on her own. And she had stayed away—more or less. But there was still a hidden memory that kept bothering her, and she hoped that taking a new look at the spring would bring it back.

She reached the spring, which still looked the same as she remembered it, and peered over the edge. Close by she could see the path she and her father had taken to get down to the cave, and it looked safe enough. That hidden memory concerning this place still disturbed her.

In a few moments she had reached the ledge that fronted the cave. Peering in, she could see that it went back into the cliff, narrowing down into a dark tunnel. Surely there could be no harm in going in for a short distance. She had no feeling of being watched from above, so she entered the cave and started back into the tunnel. Excitement rose in her. She was certain that she had been in that tunnel before—not with her father, but alone. Was she on the verge of capturing that elusive memory? It was growing darker, and she realized that she should have brought a flashlight if she wanted to do any extensive exploring. It was too dangerous to go on in the total darkness.

There was a point where another, even narrower tunnel took off to her right. It didn't look very inviting, so she continued on along the main tunnel. Soon it curved slightly, and all light from outside was cut off. No sense in going on without a flashlight, she decided. Better to come back another time.

She turned around and started back toward the entrance. Then she heard it: a scrambling noise from outside, as though someone were climbing down the side of the cliff as she had done. She paused in dismay, realizing that she had been very foolish to come in alone. It was exactly the sort of thing Brian had warned her about.

She hurried forward and in a moment reached the entrance to the dark little tunnel she had passed before. Without hesitation she crawled into it and kept going, around a bend into total darkness. It was a dead end. She came up against solid rock with only a narrow cleft in it, a cleft large enough to crawl into and lie flat, like a lizard. Well, she thought, she was trapped now, but there was a chance that whoever had followed her there might not look in this side tunnel.

The sounds of pursuit were growing louder as someone came along the main tunnel. He reached the entrance to her hideout and paused. Would he come in? Who was it—Erik's murderer? She cowered there, scarcely breathing. *The hunted is always silent when the hunter draws near,* she thought feverishly. There was a slight scuffling sound as though her pursuer had come partway into the small tunnel, and then silence.

CHAPTER SIX

Probably less than a minute passed, but it seemed much longer to Lori. Then the scuffling sound came again, as though her pursuer were backing away, and finally the sound of footsteps retreating back out of the tunnel. Apparently whoever it was had decided it wasn't worth exploring any farther.

When she felt that it was safe to leave her hiding place, she crawled out of her crevice and made her way out through the cave, climbed up the path to the top of the cliff, and headed back along the path that came out not far from the Observatory. Brian was still there, sitting on a fallen column, looking cross.

"Where on earth have you been?" he demanded

when she came up to him. He sounded just like her father. "I saw you going off into the jungle alone—"

"Not the jungle," she protested. "I merely took a walk over to the other spring. I used to go there a lot with my father."

"Well, I didn't like your going off like that alone, away from other people, so after a few minutes I followed you. I even went partway into some dark cave over there, thinking you might have been crazy enough to explore it, but you weren't there. I had to give up and come back here. Where did you disappear to, anyway?"

So it had been Brian after all, she thought. But how could she be sure that her safety had been the real reason he had followed her? Either way, she couldn't tell him that she had hidden from him. If he were innocent, it would hurt him too much to think she suspected him, and if he weren't, it would put him on guard against her suspicions. So she merely said, "Oh, I walked around the spring and back into the jungle a little, but there was nothing there, so I came back here. It was perfectly safe."

"I'm not so sure. I can see that I'd better not let you out of my sight from now on. Well, we might as well go back for lunch."

As they walked, she thought about the cave and tunnel. She was still sure there was a connection between them and that long-ago night, but what could it be? From looking at the map, she had noticed that the spring and the pyramid were not really all that far apart. She had approached it before along a path from the other side, near the hotel, but perhaps it could also be reached from the other side. Was it possible that the tunnel led to it? It would have been a good way for the priests to go in and out without being seen. Perhaps she should go back with a flashlight and follow it all the way in. It might have even been the way she had escaped from the pyramid that night if the entrance on top had been sealed. After all, the road where she had been found the next morning was not far from where they were walking now.

They were both hot and somewhat dirty after crawling around in the tunnel, so they headed for their cottages to shower before going to lunch. However, when they were passing Cottage 3, there was Mrs. Armstrong sitting on the porch wearing a brightly flowered muumuu, and she got up when she saw them and went over to the screen door. The dog was on the steps and gave them an indifferent woof.

"Miss Cahill," she called, "I've been wanting to talk to you. Would you like to stop in for a few minutes? You look as though you could use a cold drink. Both of you, I mean." She held the door open, smiling at them hopefully. Lori didn't have the heart to refuse. So they went up the steps to the porch, followed by the pug, who was letting out a series of anxious little barks.

"Oh, do be quiet, Chang," Mrs. Armstrong said. "Please sit down and I'll get some lemonade. Brian and I have already met, but we haven't been introduced, my dear. I'm Lucy Armstrong, from Lake Worth, Florida. I already know who you are—actually we did meet a long time ago, but you were just a little girl then and wouldn't remember me. I was here with my husband, but we were staying in the hotel. All the cottages were filled with your father's group. It was very exciting."

She bustled off into the cottage to get the lemonade, and Lori and Brian sat down on two plastic chairs. Mrs. Armstrong was making a big clatter getting out ice cubes at her sink, so Lori thought it safe to ask in a low voice, "Did you say she was a medium?"

He nodded. "That's right. One of those people who say they can communicate with the spirits of the dead. That's why she comes here. She says that someone she calls her control—the spirit who acts as a go-between for her and the spirits she wants to contact—was once a great Mayan priest, whose name is Tzab. Since he lived here at Chichén Itzá, she likes to visit his hometown once in a while."

"Very interesting," she murmured, but couldn't pursue the subject because Mrs. Armstrong was coming back now, carrying a tray with tinkling glasses on it as well as a plate of cookies. She set it down on the little table.

"There we are! Now you just help yourselves. I

know it's almost lunchtime, but a few little cookies won't hurt. Have you been to the ruins?"

"Yes," Lori said, gratefully taking a sip of the cold lemonade. "Brian took some pictures, and I just wandered around."

The little dog, Chang, saw the cookies and came waddling over. He sat up on his hind legs, waving his little front paws, looking more than ever like his mistress.

"Would you look at the greedy baby!" Mrs. Armstrong crooned. "Does 'ums want a yummy? Ask Mama nicely and maybe she'll give you one."

Chang let out an imperious woof, and she dropped a piece of cookie into his waiting jaws. Lori regarded the dog reflectively while it chomped, drooling all over the porch floor. It was a nasty little beast, and yet she realized that its barking had brought Brian to her rescue that first night. Or had it been Brian that had pulled the bag over her head? She didn't want to believe that.

"So you were here, too, the same year that I was?" she said, turning to Mrs. Armstrong.

"Yes. I knew your father slightly—such a fine man. I remember when you came to stay with him on your Easter vacation—such a sweet little girl, all big gray eyes and blond pigtails. Rather a tomboy too, as I recall, always out climbing around the ruins. Did you became an archaeologist too?"

"No, I'm a musician."

"Perhaps that's just as well. Much less strenuous,

I should think. We were all so shocked at what happened to you. Do you remember much about it?" She looked at Lori, head cocked on one side like an inquisitive robin.

"Very little," Lori told her. "No one would believe me when I told them that I'd seen Erik murdered."

"Well, you can't really blame them, dear. You were always making up wild tales. Erik didn't die, he just ran off to South America with some millionaire on his yacht, you know. He left a note telling what he was going to do, and his car was found in Cancun. You didn't actually *see* him being murdered, did you?"

"No," Lori admitted, "but I saw him lying there in the pyramid, all bloody with someone standing over him with a knife—"

Mrs. Armstrong leaned forward with big, excited eyes and put her hand on Lori's knee. "But did you see who it was?"

"No, he was wearing a hood, I think—I can't remember what happened after I fell down the steps."

"Oh, my dear girl, you probably just had a nightmare and walked in your sleep! And then you fell somehow and cut your head. Don't you think that might have been what happened?"

Lori shook her head stubbornly. "No, I don't. My memory up to the point where I fell down the steps is perfectly clear. It was no nightmare."

"But when you tried to take the police back to the pyramid, it wasn't there."

"You mean I couldn't find it. But it's there, I'm sure of it."

"Do—do you think you could find it again now?" Mrs. Armstrong asked doubtfully.

"I don't know, but I'm going to try."

Mrs. Armstrong looked distressed. "Do you think that's wise? If it's there, it might have a curse on it—"

"Nonsense. I don't believe in curses, Mrs. Armstrong. I want to find out if Erik's body is in that pyramid. That memory has haunted me for years, and I'd like to settle it once and for all. Believe me, no one would be happier than I would be if it turned out that Erik is still alive."

Mrs. Armstrong was silent for a moment, absently eating a cookie, and Lori could almost see the thoughts scurrying around in her untidy head. Then Mrs. Armstrong looked up and proclaimed triumphantly, "I know! We can hold a séance. I am a medium, you know. If Erik is dead, I'm sure Tzab can get in contact with him."

"Tzab?" Lori repeated blankly.

"Yes, my Control. He was once a high Mayan priest right here at Chichén Itzá—probably in the Toltec period of the eleventh century. That's why I like to come here to the source—the vibes are much stronger—although he first contacted me back in New York. That's where I lived before we retired to Florida. I used to work as a medium there, and I still do it occasionally."

"I'm sorry, Mrs. Armstrong," Lori said, "but I don't believe it's possible to contact the dead."

Mrs. Armstrong didn't seem to be offended; she merely smiled rather pityingly. "I know. Most people are skeptics at first. But won't you at least let me try? Just think how exciting it would be if Erik actually was murdered and could tell you who killed him!"

"Do they do that?" Brian asked curiously. "I mean, do victims ever actually give the name of the murderer? It would certainly save the police a lot of trouble!"

Mrs. Armstrong frowned. "Well—I've never actually known it to happen, no, but there could always be a first time. I don't suppose it would stand up in court, anyway. You can't call a spirit to the witness stand." She turned to Lori. "How about it? Will you let me try? We could have it tonight."

Lori looked at Brian, who grinned at her. "What do you think?" she asked him.

"Why not give it a try?" he said. "Sounds like great fun to me. I've always wanted to attend a séance."

"Would it be just us?" Lori asked.

"Oh, no! It takes more people to generate enough power. I'll ask some of the other cottage people. They'll probably come, even though they're skep-

tics, like you. Maybe I could even get Julian. Now
—would either of you like more lemonade?"

They turned down further refreshment, and soon
left to continue on to their own cottages.

"What do you really think about this séance nonsense?" Lori asked at her own door.

"Oh, I'm all for it," Brian replied. "For one
thing, it will get all our suspects together under
rather tense circumstances, and someone might say
or do something to give himself away."

"Just like in a mystery novel," she agreed.

"You do want to go through with it, don't you?"

"Oh, sure. Wild horses couldn't keep me away."

"Sure they could, Lori. Don't underestimate wild
horses. They can be mean—real mean! They can
keep people away from all sorts of things if they put
their minds to it."

After lunch, she decided not to go back to the
ruins with Brian. Instead she took her own car and
drove to one of the big new hotels to browse in its
gift shop. The shop had a good supply of the native
Yucatán costumes, so she bought herself one,
thinking she could wear it as an evening gown.
There were also many clay masks, which she
looked over thoughtfully.

There was one that looked vaguely familiar, and
she picked it up to examine it. Yes, she thought, it
did resemble the face she had seen at her window
the first evening. So that was what it had been—

someone wearing an Indian mask. She bought it to show Brian.

Later, when Brian had come back from the ruins and they were having coffee in her cottage, she showed the mask to him. Holding it over her face, she exclaimed, "This is what I saw looking at me through the window!"

He took it from her and examined it. "They used to put masks on the faces of dead nobles when they buried them," he told her. "This is probably a reproduction of one of those."

"So it wasn't a Chac-Mool after all, although the face is similar in expression."

"Deadpan," he agreed. "And by the way, Lori, are you aware that someone has been following you and Max around?"

She looked at him in surprise. "You've seen him? Yes, I rather suspected there was. Some man—he looks like someone out of an old gangster movie. Maybe he *is* a gangster—maybe Max has run up a big gambling debt, and he—"

"Hold it, love." Brian grinned at her. "As a matter of fact I noticed him today at the ruins. Max was sketching, and this guy was loitering around. So I took the bull by the horns and asked him why."

"Why a bull by the horns? Most bulls—oh, never mind. What did he say? Or did he deny everything?"

"No, he was quite nonchalant about it. Said he

was a private detective, paid to keep an eye on Max."

"A private eye. Did you find out why?"

"He wouldn't tell me that, but when I asked him if Max were a criminal—selling drugs or stealing artifacts—he said no, that Max was okay, a good guy. And by the way, I got his name. It's Jorge Perez. He's from San Diego."

"Mmm. I wonder if it has anything to do with my mystery, or if it's another one."

"Maybe we'll find out tonight."

After Brian left, she thought about the coming séance. She was beginning to feel more and more uneasy about it. Even though she didn't believe it was possible to contact someone from beyond the grave, she still didn't like the idea of trying. How could you know what might happen?

CHAPTER SEVEN

When they arrived at Mrs. Armstrong's cottage that evening, only her neighbor, Miss Gregory, was there ahead of them. She was in her sixties, tall and angular, with intelligent dark eyes. She told them that she was a retired schoolteacher and had been coming here for the past few years for a month every winter.

"The ruins fascinate me," she admitted. "It's such strange, desolate country here. I keep thinking about what Graham Greene said about the Yucatán —that it isn't a country to live in at all, but a country to die in and leave only ruins behind."

"Which is just what the Mayans did," Brian

agreed. "How do you feel about this séance to-night?"

"Skeptical," she replied, and smiled at her plump friend, who was wearing a wildly flowered muu-muu.

"Oh, that doesn't bother me—or the spirits," Mrs. Armstrong assured her. "I've converted many nonbelievers in my time."

Miss Gregory turned to Brian and Lori. "My theory is that the trance of a medium is a form of self-hypnosis, and that the messages received are partly from information she already has about the participants, and perhaps partly from the minds of people around her. Mental telepathy is an accepted fact, you know. That's why a medium can some-times give personal details that no outsider would know about. But this information doesn't come from the spirit of a dead person—only from the mind of a living one."

Brian nodded. "I've never attended a séance, but I've always been of the same opinion. I've heard of some mediums, though, who were completely fraudulent and had investigators uncovering ob-scure facts about their customers before they at-tended a séance."

Mrs. Armstrong smiled at them forgivingly. "That's true. I've known some like that myself, and everyone is entitled to believe as he pleases. But if poor Erik is really out there somewhere trying to contact Lori, we should give him a chance, don't you think?"

At that point Dr. Parker and Max arrived together from the main building, where they had just finished their dinner.

"Sorry if we're late," Dr. Parker said. "Service was slow in the dining room tonight."

Lori studied his face intently as they were introduced, trying to remember if she had seen him before, but nothing about him rang any bells. The man said, "I never met your father, Miss Cahill, but I'm familiar with his work. He was a very fine archaeologist. I wasn't here at the same time he was—I was in Africa that year—but I've read all his books."

"I understand you're here to do a book about the Mayans," she said, while thinking that she could eliminate him from her list of suspects. He would hardly dare to lie about his whereabouts that spring in front of someone who would know whether he had been here.

Dr. Parker shrugged. "That was my intention, but I can't seem to get started. Ought to get a few pointers from Max's boss, I suppose."

"You wouldn't like the sort of thing she does, Hank," Max said.

"But they sell like hotcakes," Dr. Parker retorted.

Lori and Brian exchanged a glance, and she knew what he was thinking: *Why hotcakes? Do they really sell better than everything else?*

There weren't enough chairs on the porch for everybody, so Mrs. Armstrong herded them all inside, saying that they had to be there for the séance anyway, and that Julian had brought over extra chairs.

Lori saw that this cottage was identical to her own. The table had been placed out in the middle of the room, with six chairs arranged around it. Mrs. Armstrong came in last, pushing Chang back onto the porch with her foot and closing the door in his anxious, wrinkled little face.

"I never let him in during a séance," she explained. "It upsets the poor baby too much. They tell me that he howls and cowers in a corner when Tzab starts talking."

Lori thought that she would probably cower in a corner and howl, too, if the spirits really came through. She hadn't been so nervous since she did her first flute solo—"The Whistler and His Dog"— at a recital when she was eight.

"Do you know what Tzab means in Mayan?" Dr. Parker asked Mrs. Armstrong.

"No, I don't believe so."

"It is the sound a rattlesnake makes before it strikes."

She looked a bit startled. "Oh? Fancy that!"

"If this Tzab of yours is an ancient Mayan priest," Miss Gregory said, "how can we understand him?"

"Oh, he speaks pretty good English, they tell me —with an accent, of course."

Miss Gregory snorted. "Oh, come now! How is that possible?"

"I suppose he picked it up after he passed over," Mrs. Armstrong replied. "After all, he's had about a thousand years to do it."

There was a tap on the door, and everyone started nervously. When Mrs. Armstrong opened it, Julian was there. "I'm sorry to be late," he said. "I was able to get away after all." He looked around at the assembled cottagers and gave them his melancholy smile.

"Oh, do come in," Mrs. Armstrong said. "I'm very happy to have you. Bring another chair from the porch, but don't let Chang in."

When Julian and the chair were safely inside, Mrs. Armstrong told them to take their places around the table.

"I never use any props," she said. "No floating trumpets, no ectoplasm coming out of a cabinet, no table tippings or raps—that's all stage-magic stuff, and the mediums that use them are fakes. I don't even use music to set a mood. We just sit around the table and hold hands—to generate the Power, you know. Then I go into a trance, and if we're lucky, Tzab will come and bring us some contacts."

She seemed to assume a new dignity as she took her place at the table, and her little pug face was remote and calm. Everyone sat down, and Lori found herself between Max and Brian. She thought that she would be glad of their protection if the going got rough. It was a round table and not very big, but they all managed to squeeze in. The shutters were closed and the light was off, with only a feeble glow coming through the cracks of the door from the security lamp outside.

When they had joined hands, Mrs. Armstrong said, "You may close your eyes or keep them open as you please. Some mediums use prayer at this point, but I have never felt that religion has anything to do with this procedure—except, of course, in the sense that the universe and everything in it are one and that all power comes from the Central Source. Try to make your minds as blank as possible."

Brian's hand was warm, and he clasped Lori's hand firmly, reassuringly. Max's was curiously cold, a little clammy, as though he were nervous— as he probably was. If the murderer were in the room, Lori thought, he was probably the most nervous of all—because whether he believed in spiritualism or not, there would be the irrational fear that the dead Erik would be summoned to accuse him!

"If Tzab comes," Mrs. Armstrong continued, "speak to him, and ask him questions if you like. That is why he is there. If there are other spirits near who wish to speak to one of us, he will produce them. I never know anything of what goes on.

My own spirit sleeps when his takes over my body and speaks through me. Don't be frightened, whatever happens—it is perfectly safe."

Lori's eyes grew accustomed to the gloom, and she could make out the dim shapes of furniture in the room. The only sounds were the gentle whir of the electric fan over their heads, the inevitable chirping of crickets, and their own breathing. Then Mrs. Armstrong's head drooped as though she had fallen asleep, and her breathing became slow and labored. After a few minutes of this, during which the tension in the room rose to an almost unbearable peak, she raised her head and began to speak. Her voice was entirely different now, no longer high-pitched and breathy but deep and sonorous and husky with an odd accent.

"This is Tzab," the voice said. "I welcome you to my homeland. The Power is strong tonight. I feel many things coming from those who are present. There is one among you I have know long ago— one whose bones lie deep in the sacred spring."

Lori had kept her eyes open, and she saw Julian's head lift sharply at that pronouncement. He had probably told Mrs. Armstrong the same story he had told her, Lori assured herself firmly.

"There are several spirits here who wish to get through," the voice continued. "I will try to let them all speak before the Power fades."

There was silence for a moment. Then a different voice, that of a woman with a definite Midwestern accent, came. "I know you're there, Henry!" the voice exclaimed angrily. "And I just want to tell you that I know all about that tomfool affair you're mixed up in. If you don't come to your senses, you're going to be mighty sorry when your time comes to join me—and at the rate you're going, that isn't going to be too long, I can tell you!"

Dr. Parker let out a strangled cry and started to rise, but Max pulled him back down. Then the voice changed, became that of a small child, singing in a little squeaky voice:

"'Twinkle, twinkle, little star, how I wonder what you are! Up above the world so high'—Mama—Mama—is that you? See, I still know the song!—'like a diamond in the sky.'"

Another muffled cry, but Lori wasn't sure who emitted it. Probably Miss Gregory, as she was the only other woman there besides Mrs. Armstrong. But Lori's contemplation was cut short by a new voice—this one a man's again, and hauntingly familiar:

"Lori—you shouldn't have come here! You're in danger! You must leave at once!"

"Daddy?" Lori gasped. "Is that you?"

"Yes—listen to me, Rabbit—Erik isn't dead—he survived and made it to South America. It was he who carried you to safety out of the pyramid. . . ."

The voice seemed to fade, and Lori cried, "But,

Daddy—if Erik is alive, who is trying to harm me? What does he want?"

"He wants the sacred serpent disk—the one who tried to kill Erik—you're in his way—go home, child—go home! The killer—he is in this room—"

As his voice rose almost to a shout, there came a loud howl from the porch, and the door burst open.

CHAPTER EIGHT

For a few minutes everything was utter confusion, as everyone jumped to his feet, knocking over chairs and milling around trying to find the light switch. Finally Dr. Parker found it and switched it on. It was only Chang, who had leaped against the door, which had not been properly latched. He was now tearing around the room letting out excited yelps. Mrs. Armstrong still sat at the table blinking and looking confused.

"What's happened?" she asked. "Why is everybody so excited?" Her eyes darted frantically from one of them to another.

Dr. Parker said angrily, "Of all the dumb nonsense—if any of you think for one minute we really

95

talked to any spirits, you're all crazy!" And he stalked out of the room.

Miss Gregory was quietly sobbing into a tissue, and she turned and fled after Dr. Parker.

Max looked angry. "I don't know what this is all about," he said, "but it seems to me you're playing a dangerous game, Mrs. Armstrong. I don't want any part of it." And he followed the others out the door.

"I'm inclined to agree with him," Julian said. "I don't think it would be advisable to speak to anyone of this episode. That talk of a killer—we don't want to start a panic in the hotel." He bowed stiffly and went out.

Lori wondered if Tzab's reference to ancient bones in the well of sacrifice had frightened him. It would certainly have reaffirmed his belief in the reality of his nightmare!

"Oh, dear!" Mrs. Armstrong lamented, gazing sadly at her two remaining guests. "I didn't mean to upset everybody. I was going to serve coffee and cookies—"

Brian patted her shoulder. "You only meant to help, Mrs. Armstrong," he said, "and we thank you for trying."

Chang whined and crawled up on his mistress's lap. She stroked his head and murmured, "Poor baby, Mama didn't mean to scare you." Then she looked up and said, "Will you please tell me what happened?"

Brian repeated what had been said as well as he could remember, with a little help from Lori.

"So!" the woman said when they had finished. "It looks as though Erik is alive after all. I'm so glad! And I'm sure you are relieved to hear it, Lori. Now you can just go home and forget about that nasty old pyramid."

"I wonder," Lori said slowly, "why Daddy didn't say who this man is who tried to kill Erik and is now after me. Wouldn't that have simplified things?"

"Not really, dear. Suppose he had said it had been—well, let's say Julian, just to pick someone at random. Wouldn't you feel you ought to do something about it? Julian would only have denied it, and it would have started all sorts of a fuss. No, better that you simply go home now, and let whoever it is go on looking for whatever it was—a serpent disk? He probably won't find it, anyway, and it all happened so long ago. . . ." Her voice trailed off, and she began to stroke the dog again, staring into space.

"We'd better go too," Brian said awkwardly, "and let you get your rest. You look done in."

"Yes, séances always exhaust me," she said faintly, "and this one was so trying."

As they walked slowly back toward Lori's cottage, Brian said, "What did you really think of all that? Did it sound like your father?"

She shook her head. "I don't know. It did and it

didn't. And after all, as she said, it was a long time ago. It was all so strange—some of the things she said must have hit home, because both Dr. Parker and Miss Gregory were genuinely upset."

"Yes, she put on a good show. But I still don't believe it's possible to talk to the dead."

"Do you think she faked it all, then? Why bother?"

"I don't know. Why should she want to convince you that you're in danger or that Erik is alive? I think her trance was genuine enough, but—as Miss Gregory suggested—the things she said either came out of her subconscious or were picked up from the minds around her. She's been coming here a lot, you know. Julian has probably told her about his nightmares, and the others may have confided in her. You'll notice that she didn't name the person who's been hounding you—probably for the simple reason that she doesn't know who it is, either."

"She mentioned something about a sacred serpent disk. Do you suppose that really exists?"

"It might have been the artifact Erik was after."

"Why didn't he take it at the time, then—if he did survive and carry me out of the pyramid, as she said?"

"If he was unconscious for a while, the other guy probably took it and ran, thinking both of you were dead."

"Then what is he doing back here now—trying to drive me away?"

"That's the part that doesn't make sense. If the thing is still there, why didn't he take it before when he had the chance? And if it isn't, why is he back here now?"

"Unless," Lori said slowly, "Erik really is dead, and it was Julian who killed him, to protect the sacred disk, and he is the one trying to keep me from finding the pyramid. Maybe he thinks *I'm* after it."

"Then why would he lead Erik to it in the first place if he didn't want him to have it?"

She sighed. "Any way you figure it, it doesn't make sense, does it? I know one thing, though— I'm not running away."

"Then you don't believe it was your father warning you."

"At the time, she had me fooled. Thinking about it now, I'm sure that if it had really been Daddy talking to me, he would have named my enemy. Anyway, he was always telling me to face up to things, not run away from them."

"What are you going to do, then?"

"Look for the pyramid, I suppose. What else can I do?"

"We'll go first thing in the morning," he promised.

She would have to trust Brian, she thought. She knew that she couldn't bring herself to go into the jungle alone. She had to trust someone, and surely her instincts couldn't be *that* wrong!

They had reached her cottage, and she turned and looked up at him in the dim lamplight. His rugged features seemed to radiate honesty and kindness. No—he couldn't be her tormentor. Not Brian.

"We'll go early," she told him, "before it gets hot. Good night, Brian."

"Good night, love. Be sure to lock your door." He bent and kissed her gently. Then he suddenly pulled her into his arms and kissed her again, this time with a fierce urgency.

"Lori—Lori—" he murmured.

She wanted to stay in his arms forever, to love him and to be loved—but she couldn't. Not yet. The image of the pyramid always intruded, a nightmare that would not go away until all the truth was revealed. So she pulled away and fled to the safety of her cottage, locking the door behind her.

She awoke early, still thinking about the pyramid, convinced that that was where the answer lay. It held the key to everything: to her memory block, to all the events of that night. With Brian's help she would find it, enter it, and discover whether Erik's body really lay there in the terrible darkness.

By the time she had dressed, Brian was there, and they went over to the hotel for breakfast. Neither of them mentioned their emotional parting of the night before, and Brian was his usual cheerful self.

"Do you still want to go pyramid hunting this

morning?" he asked when they had nearly finished eating.

"Yes, of course. It's the only thing I can do."

"But even if we find it and are able to enter it, you realize it may be empty. There has been plenty of time for the murderer—if there is a murderer— to remove both the body and the treasure."

"Then why is someone trying to prevent me from finding it?"

"He might not know that it's empty. It could be that someone else is after the treasure, someone who only suspects that it might exist and is still there."

"Don't make it any more complicated than it already is," she complained. "Actually I couldn't care less about any possible treasure. All I want is to find out whether Erik's remains are in there. If they aren't, fine. I'll go home and forget the whole thing."

"And if they are?"

"Then it's a matter for the police, isn't it?"

When they had finished, they went back to their cottages for cameras and a flashlight and set out on the path into the jungle. No one seemed to be around, and they hoped they were unobserved.

"I almost wish I had a gun," Brian said, "although I've never fired one in my life."

"Then maybe it's a good thing you don't have one," she said.

After that they didn't talk but just walked quietly

along the trail. She had no sense of being observed. Finally they came to the path branching off to the left.

"Does this look like the one?" Brian asked.

"No. Julian told me that that one leads to an abandoned village. I remember distinctly that the path we took that night was on the right."

"Do you remember how far you walked before you came to it?"

"Not exactly, but I don't think it was as far as this."

"Then the path to the pyramid must have grown shut over the years."

"Not over the years, Brian. I couldn't even find it the next day twelve years ago when I tried to lead the police there. It seemed to have vanished. There was another path a little farther on, but that one led to some other ruins. That's why they wouldn't believe me."

"Then someone must have covered it up with underbrush to throw them off. By now, though, it must be genuinely overgrown."

"I suppose so. I don't imagine the murderer has been making regular pilgrimages to it. I should think he'd avoid it like the plague."

"Why does everybody still say that, I wonder? Nobody gets the plague anymore. Nobody even thinks about it. I doubt if many people even know what it is—or was. So why maintain a cliché that dates back to the middle ages—"

"All right, all right—I agree, it's stupid. But even the best writers use it. It just sounds good somehow. What else could you say?"

"Oh, there must be lots of things we should avoid. Fire ants, for instance, or insurance salesmen or—what's that stuff we get on our teeth? Plaque. How about 'avoid it like the plaque'?"

She knew he was talking silly to keep her from brooding about the pyramid. Suddenly she realized that she was really more afraid of finding the pyramid than of not finding it. Actually she was terrified of the thing, and for two cents she'd give up the whole project and go home. Another outdated cliché. Nobody would do anything for two cents anymore. But she couldn't give up. Not when someone was so determined to make her do just that.

"I thought maybe I'd see some signs of a path, even if it is overgrown," she said, dejectedly brushing away the stinging flies that pursued her, "but I guess it's hopeless. We can't walk on through the jungle forever."

Even though it was still early, it was very warm there under the thorny trees. The sun beat down through the branches with a relentless impact.

"We shouldn't give up so easily," Brian said, looking as though he'd like to do just that. "Why don't we go on to those other ruins you were talking about? Maybe they connect with the pyramid in some way—they must have been part of the same complex."

She brightened a little. "Yes, we could do that. It isn't much farther now."

They went on, and after another ten minutes of walking, they reached another path branching off on the right. Another five minutes or so and they came out in a clearing, where they saw a small building nearly obscured by weeds. Many of its stones had fallen, but they could see the beautiful columns in the entrance, with their jaguar and rattlesnake carvings. It was a square building, with an elaborate frieze of more rattlesnakes and what appeared to be an eagle devouring a human heart. A flight of broken stairs led up to it. Inside was a single empty chamber.

They walked all around it in admiration.

"The square represented the image of heaven," Brian told her. "And the four rattlesnakes at the corners represent the four rattlers in the corners of the Mayan heaven."

"My idea of heaven is not one in which I'm surrounded by rattlesnakes!" Lori said. "But it's really a lovely building, isn't it? What a pity all this can't be restored."

"Perhaps it will be someday, but the Mexican government can't afford to do it. Is this the place you led the police to?"

"Yes, it must be. At the time I was so disappointed it wasn't the pyramid that I hardly looked at it."

"And they just turned around and left without hunting any further?"

"Yes, because I knew I hadn't walked any farther than this, and the path ended here anyway."

"So the pyramid has to be somewhere between here and the point where the other path turned off to the deserted village."

"I don't think it's very far from here, Brian. Do you see any sign of a path besides the one we came in on?"

They searched the area diligently but could find no sign of a trail that might lead back into more of the ruins.

"You might as well face it, love," Brian told her. "If the path to the pyramid has been obliterated, there's just no way you're going to find it again."

"But, Brian—I can't give up now," she protested, raising her arm to wipe away the sweat that was running into her eyebrows. "I know we're very close to the pyramid. Look, the trees aren't all that thick in here—if we head back toward the hotel through the woods instead of on the path, we might run into it—"

"And we might get so hopelessly lost nobody will ever see us again," Brian pointed out morosely.

"Oh, come on, this isn't exactly an Amazon rain forest—" She stopped abruptly, listening. "I thought I heard something!"

"There's something moving—over there in that thicket!" Brian exclaimed.

Lori backed up and clutched his arm, staring in the direction he was pointing.

The crashing sound grew louder, closer. Then the bushes were thrust aside and out stepped Julian. He was carrying a rifle over his shoulder.

CHAPTER NINE

For what seemed like a long time to Lori but was really only a brief moment, the three of them stood there motionless, staring at one another. All sorts of wild thoughts passed through Lori's mind, the principal one being that Julian had followed them there, ready to shoot them if necessary to keep them from finding the pyramid.

Then he stepped forward into the clearing and lowered the rifle so that it pointed toward the ground.

"I suppose," he said, looking at Lori, "that you are trying to find that pyramid where you claimed Erik was killed."

"That's right," she said defiantly. "I know it's around here somewhere. What are you doing here?"

He shrugged. "Hunting wild turkeys. It's a sport I indulge in occasionally when business is slack."

"Julian," Brian said, "you've lived here all your life. You must know this area as well as anyone. Is there or isn't there a pyramid such as Lori thinks she saw that night—and if there is, why didn't you or your father inform the police at the time it all happened?"

A good question, Lori thought. Looking back, she recalled that everyone at the hotel had denied all knowledge of such a pyramid—it was no wonder the police hadn't believed her.

Julian turned his sad, contemplative gaze toward Brian. He was silent a moment, apparently thinking. Then he said slowly, "I know of many ruins in here that the world has never seen, and perhaps never will. The secrets were passed down in my family. I will tell you something, but it must go no further. At one time the people who lived here in what is now the abandoned village had a secret cult —they worshiped the old gods and performed some of the old rituals, in spite of the laws the Spaniards had laid down.

"This was not in my time, you understand, or even in my father's, but my grandfather knew of it. There was such a pyramid, and it was used for the secret rituals. But then times changed—people were forced to move away, and the cult died out.

There were still a few of us, however, who knew where the pyramid was and how to open it."

"Was there a sacred serpent disk?" Lori asked eagerly.

"It was rumored so," he said, nodding. "I never went there, you understand, because my father told me of the curse that had been placed on it by the last priest to conduct the rituals there. He said that anyone who touched the sacred serpent would die. The pyramid is a tomb, you see, and a priest was buried there long ago."

"Then you must have known that Lori actually did see two men go there to rob the tomb," Brian said.

"Yes, we knew. One of our people must have betrayed the trust and led a thief there. But the curse was working—according to Lori, a man had died there—so we thought it was better to say nothing, simply to hope that they would all go away and forget that anything had happened there. As they did—until you came again." He gave Lori a reproachful glance.

"But if Erik was murdered there, the truth should be known," Lori said indignantly.

"Why? What good would it do now? The person who killed him is long gone."

"I don't think so," she said. "Unless you're the one that's been trying to keep me from finding the pyramid. Are you, Julian?"

"I've done nothing!" he protested indignantly. "I

didn't have to. You'll never find the pyramid. Someone covered the path that night, and now it has grown shut. Nobody goes there anymore. It's better that way."

"Then you won't help me find it?"

Julian shook his head."No, Lori. It's too dangerous. The curse—"

"Oh, surely you don't believe in such superstitious nonsense!" she said impatiently. "Anyway, I'm not interested in the sacred feathered serpent thing—I promise you I wouldn't touch it. All I want to know is whether Erik is in there."

"There are many things in the world that so-called civilized man simply does not understand," Julian said darkly. "It's not a question of intellectual belief, but rather one of instinct—of inherited traumas, if you will.

"It is possible that Erik found out about the disk from one of the natives who knew the secret of the tomb, and persuaded him to lead him there. Perhaps he found the treasure and fled to South America, as he said he was going to. He wasn't an admirable person. He was greedy. It's even possible that because of the object's great value, he killed the native who led him there, in order to keep all the reward for himself."

"But I saw him," Lori insisted. "It was Erik who was stabbed."

"But according to Mrs. Armstrong, he recovered and carried you to safety out of the tomb."

"All right, I'll grant you that might have happened," Lori said, "but that doesn't explain why someone is trying to frighten me away from here. You say it isn't you. So who is it?"

"Someone else who knows about the sacred disk and is trying to find the pyramid, like you," he said with a shrug.

"The person who stabbed Erik," Lori said. "But why didn't he take the disk when he had the chance?"

"I can't tell you," Julian said. "I simply don't know. But I would suggest that you do as the spirit of your father wished, and leave this place."

"I don't believe it was my father talking." She glared at him defiantly.

"Believe what you like. But one thing is certain: If you persist in wandering around in the woods like this, you are very likely to encounter a live rattlesnake, not a feathered one. They like to crawl out and lie in the ruins here during the day, and these woods are full of them."

With that encouraging pronouncement, he turned and disappeared into the underbrush.

Lori looked uncertainly at Brian. "What do you think?"

"I think he's probably right—we ought to get out of here," he replied. "Those Yucatán rattlers are mean customers."

So they started back along the path that led out of the jungle.

"Everybody is so determined to get me away from here," she complained as she walked. "But I have to find out if Erik is alive or not! I don't believe he recovered at all. In my nightmare he is lying there in the pyramid, quite dead."

"But that's only a dream, Lori," he pointed out.

"I know, but I think it's something that really happened. Otherwise, it wouldn't haunt me so. I think I was actually shut up in the pyramid with Erik's body."

"Then how did you get out?"

"I found a way somehow. You know these pyramids are supposed to have more than one entrance. If only I could remember."

"What about that millionaire—the one with the yacht? He could tell us whether Erik brought him the disk and went to South America with him."

She stopped on the path and stared at Brian. "But how on earth could I get in touch with him? That was twelve years ago. He could be anywhere—he could even be dead by now."

"Perhaps. On the other hand, he might still be coming to Mexico in the winter. I know, I know—it isn't winter anymore, but he might still be around. It wouldn't hurt to make some inquiries. I know a newspaper editor in Mérida. I'll get in touch with him and see if he knows anything about the guy—if you want me to."

She looked more hopeful. "Oh, yes, Brian! Will you? If we could only talk to him, we might find out a lot! The police should have questioned him at the time, but he'd left for South America that night, and they were so convinced there hadn't been any murder that they never bothered to get in touch with him."

"I'll call him as soon as we get back," Brian promised.

When they got back to the hotel, they were hot and tired, and Lori decided to take a quick swim in the pool while Brian was trying to get hold of his editor friend in Mérida. The cool water felt wonderful, so she swam idly around for a while, then stopped to rest in the shallow water at one end. She glanced toward the tables on the far side of the pool, and there, seated at one of the little tables, she saw the detective, wearing swim trunks and dark glasses. *Still with us,* she thought. But if he was there, could Max be far behind? The detective was never around when she was alone. Her eyes swept the area. Yes, there was Max, sitting at another table. He was also in swim trunks, and he waved when he saw Lori looking at him. She got out and walked over to him, and he stood up and pulled out a chair for her.

"How about a drink?" he asked.

"No, thanks. Too early in the day for me. How's the work going?"

"Fine. In fact I'm almost finished. I had a call from Jane last night, asking me to be back by next Monday. Some problem about the book seems to have arisen with her publisher. He wants it sooner than expected. I suppose I'll have to fly out Sunday night."

"I see." *Well,* she was thinking, *if he really is leaving so soon, then he can't be the one causing my problems.*

He was still talking. "On Saturday evening one of the big hotels is having what they call Mexican night, where everyone has to come wearing some sort of Mexican costume. It's a buffet dinner and dance. Would you like to go, Lori?"

Well, why not? she thought. It would give her a final chance to find out something about him. "Yes, I'd love to go, Max," she replied.

"Good. I'll pick you up around seven."

When she got back to her cottage, Brian was waiting for her on the steps.

"Did you get in touch with your editor friend?" she asked.

"Yes. He knew all about the guy—it seems he comes to Cancun every year. My friend has never been able to get an interview, though—the guy's as big a recluse as Howard Hughes was. But he is still in Cancun."

She sat down beside him on the steps. "If he's such a recluse, how can we get to talk to him?"

"Maybe if we told him we know where the serpent disk is, he might let us aboard his yacht."

"But we *don't* know. Anyway, he may have gotten the disk twelve years ago."

"I don't think so, or someone wouldn't be trying to keep you from finding the pyramid."

She sighed. "It's all so complicated. Just who is this man on the yacht, anyway?"

"He comes from a very wealthy old Dutch family—the Vandersloots. His parents were always gadding around the world, and they left him with his grandmother, who had an estate on Long Island. He was twenty years old when it happened."

"When what happened?"

"The event that turned him into a recluse. He was kidnapped—picked up while jogging on the beach—and the grandmother got a note demanding half a million dollars for ransom."

"Wow! Did she pay it? Obviously he was set free, since he's alive today."

"The affair was turned over to the F.B.I. and the money put in the designated spot, but they never heard from the kidnappers again."

"But this Mr. V.—how did he escape?"

"He didn't. They had buried him in a box out in the woods in a remote spot on Long Island. The box was just big enough for him to move his arms a bit, and it had a metal pipe going up through a hole to keep him from suffocating. There was a jug of water and some crackers. He was in that box for eight days."

"How awful!" To be shut up in a box, she thought, would be even worse than getting trapped in a pyramid. It was like being buried alive.

"A boy walking his dog in the woods found him," Brian continued. "The dog spotted the pipe and began to bark. The boy ran for help."

"He must have been in bad shape when they dug him up."

"Worse mentally than physically. He was in a sanatorium for several years. During that time his parents died in an accident, and his grandmother had a fatal heart attack, so he was left with a vast fortune and nothing else. He bought the ship and began his life of aimless cruising. He calls his ship *The Flying Dutchman*. He never goes ashore. He has bodyguards on board and a complete arsenal— enough to start his own revolution somewhere if he felt like it."

"How fascinating! How did Erik know about him?"

"Apparently some of the student-workers used to drive over to Cancun on weekends to live it up a bit, and Mr. V. spread the word that he would pay high prices for any artifacts they might come across. So our resourceful Erik got busy and persuaded someone—our elusive second man—to find him something."

"The black market must love Mr. V.," Lori commented dryly. "I wonder why the authorities don't get after him."

"You can get away with a lot when you're that rich. A little bribery here and there. Anyway, I understand it's all willed to various museums when he dies, so I guess they figure he's not doing any real harm."

"He sounds like quite a character. When he recovered enough to talk about it, couldn't he tell the police anything about his kidnappers?"

"I guess not. He just said that someone jumped out from behind an old boathouse and clobbered him while he was running. When he came to, he was in the box."

"I wonder why they never collected the ransom."

"I guess we'll never know. Well, what do you think? Shall we go to Cancun and try to contact him? My friend gave me a number to call there."

"Yes, I want to go. How far is it?"

"Farther than to Mérida, but not a whole lot. A little over a hundred miles. Cancun is an island, but it's connected to the mainland by a causeway or something. If we leave early, we can get there before noon."

Later that night, before she fell asleep, Lori thought of something: Suppose the detective had lied when he'd told Brian he was tailing Max—maybe Mr. V. had hired him to watch *her,* and to frighten her off if possible.

Maybe it was Mr. V. himself—in disguise—who had accompanied Erik to the pyramid, who had killed him there and taken away the disk. Now he was trying to keep her from finding the pyramid, because Erik's body was still there with the murder weapon, with his fingerprints on it.

Would she be walking into the lion's jaws by going to the yacht? It would be easy to dispose of a body—two bodies—at sea! She fell asleep to uneasy dreams.

CHAPTER TEN

In the morning, Lori's fears of the night before seemed rather far-fetched, so she decided not to mention them to Brian. In spite of everything, she still wanted to meet the strange Mr. V., even if he might be a veritable Jack the Ripper or a Mr. Hyde. At least she could establish once and for all whether Erik had sailed away on the yacht.

They got an early start off across the peninsula on Highway 180 to Cancun. Lori had dressed carefully in a demure embroidered cotton dress she'd bought on the cruise ship, and she had put her hair up in a neat chignon. Even Brian was wearing good slacks and a white sport shirt. Brian took his camera along, though he had been told that no pictures could be taken on the yacht.

He told Lori that Cancun hadn't just happened, but had been deliberately created by the government to attract tourists. It was advertised as a place where ancient kings had lived a thousand winters before, and there were indeed, he told her, ruins of pyramids and other Mayan buildings on the island.

They drove on through the town to the harbor, where there was a large white cruise ship tied up at the pier. There was also a marina full of sailing yachts and cruisers. There they found the office where they had to go to contact *The Flying Dutchman*.

At first the man operating the ship-to-shore line told them it would be impossible for them to speak to Mr. V. But when Lori asked him to explain to his employer that they had come from Chichén Itzá to talk to him about the serpent disk in the lost pyramid, he finally agreed to put the call through.

After relaying the message through what seemed to be a private secretary at the other end, he told Lori that Mr. Vandersloot would speak with her.

Mr. V.'s voice was pleasant, deep and well modulated, which rather surprised her.

"Do you actually have access to the sacred disk?" he asked.

"I'm Lori Cahill," she told him. "I was the child who followed Erik to the pyramid twelve years ago. I'd like your permission to come aboard to talk to you. I have a companion with me, Brian McDouglas, a magazine publisher. Some rather odd things have been happening to me at the ruins since I arrived a few days ago, things that I thought you might like to know about."

After a brief pause, he replied, "All right. One of my men will pick you up in the launch within a few minutes. Mr. Mirazzi, in my office, will show you where to wait for it."

She hung up and turned to Brian. "He's sending a launch."

Mr. Mirazzi pointed down toward the end of the pier. "There is a bench painted white and green," he said sulkily. "Wait there."

Apparently, Lori thought, he didn't like strangers visiting the yacht. They walked slowly down to the designated bench, where they sat and watched the boats passing by in the busy harbor. It was only a short time before a launch pulled up, a large affair with an enclosed cabin. There were a couple of men aboard, and one of them held out his hand to help Lori aboard.

They stared with great interest at the ship they were approaching; it was moored well out in the harbor. It was quite large for a private yacht, with sleek, beautiful lines. The only odd feature was its color—a silvery gray instead of the conventional white.

"Good color for a ghost ship," Brian murmured. "It matches you, Lori."

"The one in the opera had black masts and blood-red sails," she told him.

One of the things Lori disliked most was boarding a ship from a tender—a very tricky operation involving split-second timing. There was not only the up and down motion to worry about, but also the movement toward and away from the ship. Even in a calm sea it was not Lori's idea of fun, and in rough weather it could be very hairy indeed.

Fortunately this was a very calm day, and there was only a minimum of gentle heaving. A ladder had been lowered over the ship's side with a substantial platform at its base, and two sturdy sailors were waiting to grab them as they jumped for it. Lori went first and felt herself grabbed with a grip that she was sure would leave bruises on her arms for days as they hauled her over. Brian came close behind.

By now she was beginning to feel extremely jittery over the prospect of meeting the mysterious Mr. V. Suppose she took one look at him and realized that he had been the person in the pyramid with Erik! What would she do? Scream, leap overboard, and start swimming for shore? Or control herself and say nothing at all? She should have discussed that contingency with Brian. Well, it was too late now. She'd have to play it by ear and hope for the best.

A man was waiting to greet them on the deck. Giving them a stiff little bow, he said that he was

Albert Munro, Mr. Vandersloot's private secretary. He was around Brian's age—short, a bit stocky, with thinning, curly dark brown hair and thick-lensed glasses with heavy black frames. He seemed to have a habit of curling his lips back from his teeth in a meaningless grimace that Lori found irritating. She'd once known a dog that did that. She didn't like his hands, either; they were thick fingered and hairy. She always noticed hands.

He made a little speech of welcome, then said he was sorry but he would have to search them for weapons and cameras. He had a faint foreign accent that Lori couldn't place. Lori handed him her canvas bag, which he went through, and then his eyes glided over her body as though he thought she might have a dagger strapped to her thigh. How awful, she thought, for a man to live like that, constantly expecting some sort of attack.

When he searched Brian, he did check his pockets and turned up the little camera Brian had hoped to smuggle aboard.

"I'm sorry, sir," Albert said, "but no cameras are allowed. I'll hold it in my office for you."

She could see that Brian was annoyed, but there was nothing he could do about it. They had come aboard on the Promenade Deck, which housed the main lounge, and it was there that they were promptly escorted. When Albert pushed open the swinging doors, they were greeted by the strains of Mozart's Symphony in G Minor, which calmed

Lori down instantly. She hadn't realized until that moment how much she'd missed music. She had grown up constantly surrounded by it and had come to take it for granted—a part of the environment, like air. Since coming to Chichén Itzá she'd unknowingly been suffering from withdrawal symptoms. Now she realized how badly she'd needed a Mozart fix. A flood of joy surged through her.

Mr. V. had to be all right, she thought, if he listened to Mozart. Nevertheless her knees felt a bit weak as she and Brian were led through the lounge, which was luxuriously furnished, toward a smaller room at the back.

"Mr. Vandersloot is in the library," Albert told them. "I will see if he is ready to receive you." He left them standing in the lounge.

Lori and Brian looked at each other, but didn't dare speak for fear of being overheard. In a moment Albert was back, rolling his lips at them in what he presumably intended as a smile.

"You may go in," he said and held the door open for them.

Lori went first, and just before she stepped over the threshold she felt a strange urge to cross herself —which was weird, because she wasn't a Catholic and didn't even know how. She drew a deep breath and walked into the library.

The room they entered was fairly small, its walls completely covered with shelves of books behind glass doors. In the center was a gleaming mahogany desk, and behind the desk, rising as they approached him, was Mr. Vandersloot. Lori's first reaction was one of relief, for she realized at once that he couldn't have been the second man at the pyramid; he was a small man, very slight of build, with pale blond hair and rather ordinary features— except for his eyes. With a shock of dismay she saw that they were pale blue and quite dead looking, blank and expressionless, like the gaze of the Chac-Mool.

She took the hand he held out, and it was cold and dry. She looked into those dead eyes, and it was like looking into still, opaque water.

"Miss Cahill," he said, "and Mr. McDouglas. Welcome aboard." He indicated two chairs drawn up before the desk. "Please be seated."

They all sat down and looked at one another. As she had noted on the phone, Mr. V.'s voice was attractive although rather expressionless. He was dressed informally in slacks and a sport shirt, with the addition of an antique-looking gold chain around his neck and, on one finger, a gold ring that seemed to have the head of some god on it. "Would you like some coffee?" he asked. "I'm sorry I can't offer you anything stronger, but I don't allow alcohol on the ship."

"Coffee would be fine," Lori said, wondering what he had against drinking. Many people who had gone through an experience like his would have become heavy drinkers, she would have thought, but perhaps he strove for constant equilibrium in his life—no ups, no downs. She was beginning to feel depressed; the ship had an unhealthy atmosphere.

Apparently Mr. V. had pressed an invisible button, because a tall dark man glided in with a tray containing fresh coffee, cups, and a plate of fancy pastries. While she was drinking her coffee, Lori tried to analyze her reaction to Mr. V. Even though he did not seem quite human, there was no evil in him, she felt sure of that. He was strange but nonthreatening.

"I'm sorry we had to confiscate your camera," Mr. V. said to Brian, "but I find it a necessary rule. As you no doubt are aware of my past history, you must realize I've had enough attention from the media to last me a lifetime. As for the liquor, I'm not particularly against drinking—I like a glass of good wine now and then—but it has been my experience that drinking breeds trouble. And since it is my aim to keep life on my ship as simple and peaceful as possible, I have made that another rule. The weapons, of course, are obvious."

"I understand," Brian replied. "Actually I had no intention of using any pictures of your ship in my magazine. I'm simply an inveterate photographer, and I take snaps wherever I go."

"But one can never be sure where an innocent snapshot might end up or into whose hands it might fall," Mr. V. pointed out blandly. "The sums of money offered by some of the less-savory newspapers or magazines for a picture of me and my ship would tempt the most well-intentioned person."

The strange, zombielike eyes now turned upon Lori. "So you are the child that was found wandering on the road the day after Erik disappeared," he said. "I read an account of it in a paper later on. A curious affair, I must say."

Lori leaned forward eagerly. This was what she had come to hear. "You say 'disappeared,'" she said. "Does that mean that you didn't see Erik that night? That he didn't sail to South America with you?"

"If anyone had taken the trouble to ask me," he replied, "I would have told them that I did not see Erik, that he did not deliver the artifact as promised, and that he certainly did not sail with me."

Lori threw Brian a triumphant look. "And nobody showed up in his place?" she asked.

"No, no one. I can't imagine who drove his car to Cancun and abandoned it there, although I suppose it might have been the person who accompanied him to the pyramid. But if that person killed him to get the disk for himself, why didn't he bring it to me for the money I had offered? So far as I know—and I have very good sources of information—that disk has never been seen or offered for sale anywhere."

"That's what I've been trying to figure out," Lori admitted. "Unless it was a religious fanatic who wanted the disk to remain where it was."

"But from what little Erik told me, the person who found the disk and was going to take him to the pyramid was not a simple native but someone who made a living by smuggling out artifacts. I can understand that he might have double-crossed Erik and killed him in order to have the money all to himself—but if so, why didn't he show up here to collect the money? If he had sold it elsewhere, I would have heard."

"And why didn't he just sell it to you directly in the first place?" Brian interjected. "I mean, why drag Erik into it at all?"

"Perhaps because only Erik had talked to me and knew that I was willing to buy the disk. This other man had sold only to a dealer back in Miami, and no large sums of money were ever involved. Be that as it may, I would still like to have the disk for my collection. That is why I allowed you to come aboard—because you professed some knowledge of it." His eyes moved quickly from one of them to the other. "Do you know where it is?" he demanded. "Could you get it for me?"

"No," Brian admitted, "we've been trying to find the pyramid, but there seems to be someone who doesn't want us to. Lori has had quite a bit of harassment since she arrived."

"Is that so?" He eyed her contemplatively. "That means the other man is at present in Chichén Itzá. A very mysterious affair indeed. I'm disappointed that you can't get the disk for me. But in case you do find it, my offer remains open. Would you like to see my collection?"

They both said eagerly that they would, so he rose from the desk, opened a concealed door behind it, and led them into another room, this one without windows. It was perhaps twelve by fifteen feet in dimension, and its walls were completely covered by artifacts—some in glass-fronted cabinets, some on open shelves, some hanging on the walls. There were carved gods and goddesses, weapons, household utensils, jewelry, grave masks, and just about anything imaginable that might have come from the far past. He led them around, giving the history of some of his favorite items. Lori was impressed. Obviously this collection was worth a great fortune.

"It's a marvelous collection," she told him. "I wish my father could have seen it."

Mr. V. smiled. "He might have admired it, my dear, but he would hardly have approved of my methods of obtaining it."

"Was it all acquired through the black market, then?" Brian asked.

"Yes, I must confess, they were all acquired illegally. Do you think that very wicked of me, Miss Cahill?"

She shrugged. "As the young woman said in *Die Fledermaus*," she replied, "'Our motto has always been—*Chacun son goût!*'"

The man threw back his head and laughed at that. "Very broad-minded of you. But I assure you, all my treasures will go back to their respective countries at my death, so I can't feel very guilty about them—unless"—he sobered suddenly—"my acquisition of them has inadvertently led to someone's death."

"Dangling large sums of money in front of people who have nothing is always dangerous," Brian said. "How did you happen to get involved with Erik, anyway?"

Mr. V. sighed. "It was a mistake. I realize that now. I should have stayed with my usual sources. As you know, I am interested in ancient artifacts of the Meso-American civilizations. I had heard about the interesting finds that had been made at the Well of Sacrifice and longed to obtain something from there.

"When I arrived here twelve years ago in the late winter and learned that there was a group of students working with archaeologists at Chichén Itzá and that some of the students often came to Cancun, I invited them aboard my ship. When I sounded them out about artifacts, Erik was the only one who seemed interested. He said he knew a man there who had a way of getting artifacts from somewhere in the jungle. He said if he could offer him enough money, he might persuade him to get something for me.

"Later he came again and showed me a snapshot of the golden feathered serpent disk and said that the man wanted to know what he would give him for it. I knew this was a very valuable find indeed and offered him three hundred fifty thousand dollars."

"It's probably worth more," Brian said.

"Of course, but it would be difficult to smuggle out, being so large, and the Mexican government would certainly claim it if they found out about it. Anyway, Erik said he would get the man to take him to the pyramid where it was hidden, and they would both bring it to me here to collect the money. Erik asked me if I would take him to the next port of call in South America, and I agreed because I was very eager to obtain the disk.

"The night they were supposed to come here with it arrived, but no one appeared. I waited all night, but in the morning I heard that there had been some sort of trouble about an injured child who claimed she had seen Erik murdered, so I ordered the ship to sail. I have wondered ever since what really happened, so naturally when you showed up, I wanted to talk to you." The strange eyes regarded Lori for a moment; then he asked, "And what is your profession, Miss Cahill?"

She smiled demurely. "One of the world's oldest, I imagine." When he looked rather startled, she added, "I'm a flute player."

He laughed. "Indeed, they do go back rather far. And where do you play this flute? Not in some wooded glen, I should imagine."

So Lori explained what she had been doing and

what her prospects were for the future. Whenever he turned those pale eyes on her, she felt a strange little pang of dismay, and yet she wasn't in the least afraid of him.

They went back out to the main lounge, which was a very luxurious room, with soft, deep couches around the walls and some small tables of fine, polished wood. An Oriental carpet of deeply glowing colors covered the floor, and on the walls were some Dutch Master paintings, which she supposed were originals. Silky dark curtains were drawn over the windows.

Now there was a young woman sitting on one of the couches, smoking a cigarette. She had an exquisitely beautiful face, a cloud of dark hair, and great dark eyes. Lori noticed that even shipboard she was wearing pumps with very high heels. She looked South American to Lori.

Mr. V. introduced her as his "companion," Felicia Gamboa, and Lori reflected that although he had eliminated weapons, liquor, and cameras from his ship, he still permitted sex, which throughout history had caused as much trouble as drinking.

Brian was looking at her, and she knew he was thinking the same thing she was: *Let's get off this ship as fast as we can.* Well, she had found out what she'd wanted to know—that Erik had never shown up on that fatal night—so she might as well go. Mr. Vandersloot turned to her and said:

"Miss Cahill, I must repeat my offer. If you really think you can find that pyramid again—"

"No!" she said more sharply than she'd meant to. "Forget it, Mr. Vandersloot. That disk has caused enough trouble already. And anyway, while you may not object to buying contraband goods, I have no intention of selling you any. It's illegal—and I understand Mexican jails are rather nasty. If the disk is ever removed from there, it should go to the anthropological museum in Mexico City."

He made a little resigned gesture. "You are right, of course, my dear. I did want it very badly, but I can see that I must resign myself to failure. What do you intend to do now?"

"I still want to find the pyramid. I think Erik's body is in there. I have always been convinced that he was killed that night."

"Probably he was, or he would have come to me. But I don't quite understand why you came back to Chichén Itzá after all this time if you're not after the disk. You were only a child, and your acquaintance with Erik was brief and superficial. Why does it concern you so much now what happened to him?"

Lori hesitated a moment, and then explained, "Because I still get nightmares about that night." She went on to describe them to him, and when she reached the part about awakening in the total darkness of the tomb, he gave her a look that chilled her blood.

"Then you know," he whispered. "You know! So few people understand what it is like. . . ."

"Yes," she said gently. "I know."

He reached out and touched her hand with his cold, dry fingers. "It is the ultimate horror," he said. "But tell me the rest of it."

When she had finished, he was silent for a few moments. Then he shook his head. "Very strange," he said. "I wonder how you got out. You will probably never know the whole story."

"Maybe not, but I'm trying to find out."

"But if it is dangerous for you there, you really shouldn't stay."

Lori sighed. "That's what everyone tells me, but I'm not going to run away."

"You are a brave but foolhardy young woman," he said. "And now perhaps you would like to be shown to a cabin where you can rest before lunch. You have had a long drive."

Again Brian and Lori exchanged glances. "If you don't mind," she said, "I think we'll start back now. We don't want to impose on you any more than necessary. You have been very kind."

She knew that she might regret later that she hadn't spent more time on the ship when she had the chance, but something about the atmosphere of the place disturbed her, and Mr. V. himself, while she honestly liked him, was not a comfortable person to be around. You could never tell what went on behind those pale, dead eyes.

"All right, if that is your wish. But you are welcome to stay."

A short while later, as they sped toward shore, Lori looked back to where he stood on the deck, still watching them. He looked small standing there —and very lonely.

CHAPTER ELEVEN

They didn't talk much on the drive back to Chichén Itzá. Lori dozed occasionally and thought about what she had learned from Mr. V.

"What did you think about him?" she asked Brian finally. "Is he crazy or just a bit eccentric?"

"Mad as a hatter," Brian said cheerfully, "and I wonder how *that* cliché originated. Were hatters all mad at one time?"

"I think it had something to do with the material they made the hats out of," Lori said. "Some chemical or substance that made them a bit batty. I got the feeling that part of him is still buried in that box—and I can understand that, because I've felt

136

something of the sort about the pyramid for a long time."

"But you didn't withdraw from the human race," Brian pointed out. "What a life! You'd think he'd get cabin fever. And how about that Felicia! Did you notice she never said anything? I wonder what language she speaks—if any."

"Probably something pre-Columbian," Lori said. "Anyway, now we know Erik didn't go to South America. So I was right—his body has to be in the pyramid."

"Unless it was removed later. Lori, don't you think it's about time you went to the police and asked their help in finding the pyramid? If you told them about the gold disk, they might be more anxious to cooperate."

"Maybe. I'll think about it. You know, I'm sure Julian knows where the pyramid is, but he won't tell. It's as though he wants to protect it. Do you suppose he could have been the one who stabbed Erik in the pyramid that night? Maybe he did it to protect the disk. He's a rather odd guy, and he might have some strange ideas about ancient Mayan rites. And he really thinks he's a reincarnation of a child who was thrown into the *cenote* a long time ago."

"It's possible," Brian conceded. "And he's been around whenever anything has happened to you—

except for the time you nearly fell into the Well of Sacrifice. We know he didn't push you."

"I'm beginning to think that that was a separate incident and that nobody pushed me deliberately," she said. "And yet—it was an odd coincidence if so, and I don't trust coincidences."

"They do happen, though. Well, you can decide tomorrow what you want to do next."

The following day she still hadn't made up her mind about going to the police, and since Brian wanted to spend one more day photographing the ruins, she decided just to take it easy, sunning and swimming.

That evening, after Brian had come back to his cottage and cleaned up, he went over to Lori's cottage. "I heard that they're having a special Mexican night at one of the hotels," he told her. "Would you like to go?"

Lori looked at him blankly. The affair of *The Flying Dutchman* had wiped everything else out of her mind.

"Oh, no, that's right!" she said. "I forgot all about it. I told Max I'd go with him. I was going to wear my *huipil*."

Brian looked at her indignantly. "I thought you were through with him."

"Not quite," she said. "He's one of the loose ends I'd like to tie up. Maybe if I go out with him one more time, I can find out why a detective is shadowing him."

"Every time I want to take you someplace special for dinner, that guy has gotten to you ahead of me," he said, looking like a sulky little boy.

"*C'est la vie,* chum," she told him, and went off to shower.

When Max showed up at her door later that evening, she had been expecting to see him dressed as a *caballero,* with boots and a sombrero and so forth. Instead he was wearing the simple loose white tunic and trousers of the peon. The only touch of color was a vivid red sash. He looked absolutely smashing, and Lori gazed at him in awe.

"You look incredible!" she said.

He laughed. "That was supposed to be my line. I thought this would match your *huipil.* It's very becoming, Lori."

Lori had rather thought so herself. She smiled at him, picked up her little evening purse, and slipped her arm through his. She wondered if Brian was watching from next door.

They drove off in Max's rented car. It was about a mile over to the other hotel, which was not near the ruins but farther up the highway. It was one of the newer ones, all white stucco and gleaming tiles and lush gardens. *Nothing dingy or crumbling about this one,* Lori thought, *but give it a few years.*

"This place looks awfully new," she commented as they entered the big lobby full of potted palms.

"I believe it's about two years old," Max said, looking around. "If Jane had been able to come, we'd have stayed here. She likes luxury. But I preferred the idea of having my own cottage. More room to spread my gear around."

They went on to the dining room. Most of the other diners also wore Mexican costumes in anticipation of the ball to follow. Some of them were exceedingly elaborate. There was a group of mariachi singers to entertain them while they ate, and they were very good, singing and playing their guitars with the usual verve and precision.

There were a few Mayan artifacts—probably imitation—stuck around in deference to the location, but on the whole it could have been any hotel in any posh tropical resort, and heaven knew Lori had seen enough of them.

On the first floor there was a ballroom with a beautiful tiled floor and arched doorways opening onto a terrace, which overlooked a small lake with a fountain in the middle and lush vegetation all around. Small parrots were flitting among the trees. Very exotic. The affair had attracted a good crowd, and Lori enjoyed watching the tourists in their varied costumes.

She noticed that all the women gave Max the eye as they went past, and she supposed it had always been that way with him. To give him credit, though, he didn't seem to notice their admiring stares. She finally spotted Perez—the detective—

off in a corner of the ballroom. He was wearing a Mexican bullfighter's costume, of all things, and looked quite authentic.

There was a little orchestra playing romantic music for the dancers, and Lori felt a brief, nostalgic twinge for her old ensemble. This was the sort of thing they had done so well. Tonight, she thought, perhaps she could find out what the mysterious barrier was between her and Max. Not that she had any desire to break through it, she told herself—she was just curious.

At one end of the room a bar was dispensing drinks, and there were little tables on the terrace, where the guests could sit if they tired of dancing. Lori wondered if a few drinks would loosen Max's tongue and make him reveal some of his secrets. However, he wasn't much of a drinker and seemed to prefer dancing.

A new couple appeared in the main entrance as they danced by, and Lori's glance slid casually over them—then came sharply back in a double take. The man was tall and slender and was dressed exactly like the waiters at the Hotel Kukulcan. He also sported a sombrero and a drooping black mustache, which was slightly askew.

The girl with him was a lush little brunette, obviously a real Mexican, in a gorgeous ruffled dress of the sort dancers wear. Her dark eyes sparkled as she gazed around the ballroom, and she clutched her companion's arm possessively. Lori stared at them in disbelief. It couldn't be—but it was!

Max was regarding her quizzically. "What's the matter, Lori?" he asked. "You look like you've just seen a ghost."

"Sure," she muttered, "a ghost with a crooked mustache. Do you know that couple, Max?"

He looked back over his shoulder. "Hmm. I think I've seen the girl before—she's a dancer from one of the other hotels. But the man? Silly-looking clod, isn't he? No, I don't think I know him."

The idiot! Lori thought furiously. How dare he follow her here like that, and where did he get that stupid mustache? And where had he picked up that girl? She felt a pang of unreasonable jealousy, and then she was swept by a tide of love so intense that she knew that whatever happened she was totally committed to that crazy, wonderful man. Then the funny side of it hit her, and she had to choke back a fit of giggles. She looked at Brian again, and he was staring at her intently. The mustache had slipped a few more degrees.

"At least it isn't the man who's been following me around," Max said. "I haven't seen him to-night."

"I have," Lori told him. "Over there by the bar."

Max glanced over and made a sound of annoyance. Perez was leaning against the bar, sipping a drink and regarding them with a bored expression.

"Come on, Lori," Max said angrily. "Let's get out of here. This is getting ridiculous."

"Where to?"

"Oh, anywhere. Out in the garden."

Well, that was all right, she thought. Maybe she could get him to talk to her. Probably their two spies would follow them out, but that couldn't be helped.

They went outside, past the people sitting at the tables on the terrace, down the broad steps, and along one of the neatly tiled paths into the lush garden. Max led her to a bench on the far side of the lake. There was plenty of shrubbery around for their spies to hide behind, Lori noted, but so far she saw no sign that they had been followed into the garden.

Max put one arm along the back of the bench behind Lori, and gazed moodily at the lake. There were colored lights strung up along the path in the trees, so it was not very dark. The moon was showing over the top of the palm trees and faint strains of music floated down from the ballroom. No one could ask for a more romantic setting, Lori mused, and here she was with a man as handsome as any out of one's wildest daydreams—

She should have been enthralled, entranced, aquiver with emotion—but she felt nothing. It was like a stage setting without any reality, and all she could think of was Brian and that sexy Mexican girl.

"Max," she said, determined not to waste her opportunity, "do you know of any reason why someone would put a tail on you?"

He sighed. "Yes, I guess so."

"Do you feel like telling me about it?"

He leaned forward with his elbows on his knees. "If I told you the truth, you'd never want to speak to me again," he said morosely.

"Oh, come on!" she protested. "It can't be as bad as all that."

"It is, though. You must have wondered why I didn't try to make a pass at you the other night."

"The question did enter my mind, yes."

"It wasn't that I didn't want to—you must know I'm crazy about you, Lori. But whatever I feel, it's no good. I'll just have to go away and never see you again."

"I wish you'd tell me why. Do you have a wife in an asylum? Are you entering a monastery in a few weeks? Please don't keep me in suspense!"

"It's worse than any of those. If I told you, you'd look at me with those beautiful silver eyes full of scorn—"

"Oh, come off it, Max! Nothing could be that bad—unless maybe you've been stealing the life savings of little old ladies—"

"What an imagination you have, Lori. You ought to write books." He sighed. "All right, I'll tell you, but you'll probably wish I hadn't."

"I don't think so. I'm fairly broad-minded. And I

believe that it's always best to know the truth about things."

"I'm not sure I agree with that, but you asked for it, so here it is." He heaved another sigh, then went on in a flat, factual tone: "When I was twenty, I went to L.A. and took an art course, doing TV commercials to pay my way. In those days I still thought I could paint. I wouldn't have minded getting into films, but aside from my looks I had no particular talent for acting, either. I was invited to a lot of parties and met a lot of people. It was at one of the parties that I met Jane."

"The woman you work for."

"Yes. Jane was from one of those old California families with tons of money. But she was never the playgirl type; she was very studious and hard-working. Arrogant and self-willed, too, the way rich people usually are, but she was interesting, and I liked her."

"And she liked you, obviously."

"Yes. She invited me out to her beach house, and it wasn't long before she asked me if I'd like to move in with her. She made me a pretty good offer, so I decided to take her up on it. Besides an allowance, she puts a certain amount in a special bank account for me. When we break up, I'll get what's there. Naturally, the longer I stay with her, the more I'll get."

"And she lets you illustrate her books to give you something to do."

"I told you you wouldn't like it," he said morosely.

"Max, I really don't care how you make a living. But didn't you ever want to get married and have a family?"

"Not particularly. I just want to live in comfort and reasonable luxury, and Jane has made that possible. I'm very grateful to her, and I was perfectly happy—until I met you."

"Aren't you afraid you might jeopardize your security by taking me out?" she asked coldly.

"No, she said it's all right to take a girl out to dinner and dancing, that sort of thing, but no sex. She's very fastidious about that. One misstep and I'm out cold, without any money. That's never bothered me before. I've never been much interested in chasing women, maybe because I've had them chasing me all my life. It sort of turned me off sex. But I get along fine with Jane."

"So she hired a detective to keep an eye on you."

"I guess so. We've never been apart before, and she never takes chances. Well, now you know. Aren't you going to denounce me or something?" He seemed disappointed at her lack of reaction.

"I'm sure there isn't anything I could say that you haven't already said to yourself. It's your life. If the setup suits you, fine."

"You wouldn't understand," he said in a choked voice, "what it's like to come from a large family without any money—a drunken father— Well, I

won't go into that. I ran away as soon as I could.
Swore I'd make something of myself. I know you
think I'm a weakling—"

"Oh, come off it, Max. You don't have to justify
yourself to me."

"Yes, I do, Lori, because I've fallen in love with
you. You're different from anyone else I've ever
known. I was going to stay with Jane until the bank
account got up to a million, but—"

"A million! How long would that take?"

"About ten more years, I guess." He put his arms
around her. "Lori," he said, almost stammering, "if
I said I was willing to give up Jane and the money
—would you marry me?"

Lori looked at him in amazement. She hadn't
dreamed he was that serious. "Let me get this
straight," she said. "Are you offering to throw over
Jane and her million dollars if I say I'll marry you?"

He looked confused. "I don't know. I'd have to
think about it. But in order to decide, I need to
know if you would marry me if I gave up Jane. I
think that with you I could become a real person
and make something of myself on my own. If only
you cared for me. . . ."

It was the strangest marriage proposal she'd ever
had. "Max," she said, "I'm flattered that you are
weighing me against a million dollars—I never realized I was worth so much. But honestly, I'm
afraid you don't have any idea what love is all
about. You're better off sticking with Jane, believe

me. I'm sure you'll be happier with your million dollars than you'd ever be with me. You have quite a few years behind you now—hang in there."

"I suppose it's that guy you've been going around with," he said gloomily, "though what you can possibly see in him, I can't imagine. He—"

At that moment there was a rustling in the bushes behind them, and Lori jumped up, swinging around in an automatic reaction. The clump of bushes was perhaps ten feet behind the bench, and back among the large clusters of leaves she saw a robed figure with the same face that had looked at her through the window her first night in the cottage. It raised its arm, and she saw the dull gleam of a knife.

CHAPTER TWELVE

Instinctively Lori threw herself to the ground as the knife went whooshing over her head and fell into the lake. Max let out a cry of astonishment and went dashing off into the bushes after the apparition. At the same time another figure charged out of the bushes some distance away and ran along the path toward her: a tall man with a silly mustache that seemed in imminent danger of falling off.

"Lori!" he cried. "Are you—" Then his foot slipped on the tiles, and with a wild yell he toppled into the lake. Lori ran over to the edge and peered in. His head quickly popped up—minus the mustache, but with a fetching headdress of water lilies. He made a remark that she pretended not to hear.

149

"While you're in there, Brian," she told him, "feel around and see if you can find the knife that somebody threw at me—there's a good chap."

He glared at her, pulled off the lilies, and started to grope around on the bottom of the lake, which was only a couple of feet deep. After a few minutes he waded toward her, triumphantly holding up a dripping object.

Lori took it from him and examined it as he climbed out. It was one of those daggers sold in great numbers to tourists—an imitation of a sacrificial knife, with a jade handle carved with Mayan gods. It was not very sharp and would probably not have inflicted any real damage. *Another attempt to intimidate,* she reflected, *not to kill.*

The Mexican girl Brian had brought came hurrying along the path, but when she saw Brian she stopped in horror, yelled something at him in Spanish, turned on her heel, and went back to the hotel. Max came out of the bushes empty-handed.

"He got away," he said. "Just disappeared into thin air." Then he saw what she was holding and cried, "Lori, you might have been killed!"

"No," she said, "I don't think so. This thing is hardly lethal."

"We should call the police," Max went on. "You can't ignore something like this!"

"Yes, I can, just like I've ignored everything else. What could we show them? A toy dagger?" She turned to Brian. "You've got to get out of those wet clothes. Whatever possessed you to come here in such an outfit?"

He stood there sadly, trying to wring water out of his jacket. "I borrowed it from one of the waiters at the hotel. I guess it's ruined now, so I'll have to pay him for it. The girl was his sister. She's a dancer or something. I just thought I ought to be here to keep an eye on you."

"A lot of good that did!"

"I know, but I tried." He sloshed miserably away.

"I think we'd better go home too," Lori told Max, "before anything else happens."

At the door of her cottage he said, "So much for my romantic attempt. I suppose this is good-bye. I'm going to drive to Mérida in the morning. If I thought there was really any chance for me— Lori, would it be any use for me to get in touch with you later?"

She looked at his intent face by the light of the porch lamp, but she knew that when he got home to Jane and the security and luxury he was used to, all this would be forgotten. She leaned over and kissed him gently on the cheek.

"Good-bye, Max," she said.

For another moment he looked into her eyes; then he turned and walked slowly away. She went on into her cottage and was just starting to slip out of her costume when Brian knocked on her door and came in. He had changed into shorts and a sport shirt. For a moment they just looked at each other. Then she went into his arms.

"Oh, Lori!" he murmured into her hair. "I love you so much—"

"I love you too, Brian," she replied softly, her cheek against his chest.

"Will you marry me?"

"Of course, when all this is over—"

He held her away so that he could look into her eyes. "Lori, you know we're not getting anywhere. Somebody wants to get rid of you. Okay, let him have his way. Let's just chuck it and leave tomorrow."

It was tempting. So very tempting that she almost said yes. But then the vision of Erik in the pyramid came back, and somehow she had a feeling that the answer was just around the corner, waiting to be revealed.

"I'm sorry, Brian," she said, "but I can't just chuck it now after all I've gone through."

"But Lori—"

"No, wait," she said, pulling away from him. "I'm willing to compromise, but I won't give up. I'll admit I'm not getting anywhere on my own, so tomorrow I'll go to the police and tell them everything I know—everything that's happened since I came here. I'm pretty sure that if I tell them about the gold disk, they'll take more interest. Surely if they make a real effort, they can find that pyramid."

"Now you're being more sensible, love. By all means, let the police handle it. And if they do find Erik's body, they'll have to investigate, and maybe they'll turn up his murderer, since he still seems to be around. So no more poking around on your own —right?"

"Right!" she agreed and went back into his arms.

Later, when he had returned reluctantly to his own cottage, she locked all the windows, the screen door, and the door into the cottage. But then it was too stuffy, so she opened the window over her bed. If anybody tried to come through the screen, she'd just yell for Brian.

Finally she went to bed. Although she was tired and it was quite late, she couldn't sleep. She had too many things on her mind. She thought about the pyramid. She had always been sure that if she ever entered it again, all the memories of that night would come back. She might even know the identity of the figure with the knife— She shivered, and her eyes went to the kitchen table, where the knife that Brian had fished out of the pool was laying.

Had the same hand that had killed Erik thrown that one? If so, would it have fingerprints on it to reveal his identity? But perhaps they had been washed off in the water. And then, of course, she and Brian had both handled it. The police were very clever at that sort of thing. . . .

Tired as she was, she simply couldn't shut out the thoughts that crowded into her mind. Her usual

ploy when she couldn't sleep was to go over musi-
cal scores in her head, but now she couldn't even
concentrate on that.

What was causing such deep unease? Probably it
was simply that too much had been happening too
fast and she'd overloaded her circuits. She turned
onto her back and forced herself to relax, lying very
quietly. It wasn't long before she realized that instead of relaxing, she was listening—to what? Was
anyone out there, moving stealthily around? She
thought she heard a faint click—as though someone had closed the gate leading into the jungle.

Leaping off the bed, she ran into the bathroom
and peered out the back window, from which it was
just possible to see the gate. In the bright moonlight
she was almost sure she saw a dark figure moving
off down the path. She knew without question that
it was the person who had killed Erik and who had
been plaguing her ever since her arrival. All
thoughts of going to the police were forgotten now,
and even the idea of waking Brian did not occur to
her. There was no time for anything, only to follow
that elusive figure before it disappeared into the
jungle and was lost forever.

She pulled on shorts and a T-shirt, slipped into
her sneakers, and let herself out through the screen
door. No one seemed to be around; after all, it was
after one o'clock in the morning. She ran around
the cottage and back toward the gate, then through
it onto the path. She hadn't taken time to find her

flashlight, but the moon was out, and even in the jungle she could see fairly well. She was more familiar with the path now, and she almost ran for a while, but soon had to slow down because she was getting out of breath. She vowed that if she ever got out of this, she'd get up every morning at six and jog for an hour.

She didn't dare let herself think about what might be ahead, and she kept out fear by concentrating on keeping an even pace and being as quiet as possible. She didn't relish the thought of a possible ambush. The figure hadn't had much of a head start, so he couldn't be very far ahead. She was moving so quickly that she almost went past it before she noticed it was there: a new path, apparently freshly cut, off to the right of the main path.

She didn't doubt that this was the path to the pyramid or that the figure she was following had turned off here. She entered the path far more slowly than she had been moving before. No need to hurry now—she knew where her enemy had gone. The path was narrow, only wide enough for one person to walk. From her memory of that night twelve years before, it was not very far after she turned off the main path—barely a city block.

She came out of the jungle into a little clearing, much smaller than she remembered it, as the underbrush had obviously been cut down very recently. There it stood in the moonlight, almost obscured by the weeds and grasses that had grown over it. The pyramid was still a moving sight, with its intricate carvings of jaguars, eagles, and snakes around its base. Rising to a height of about thirty feet, it was much smaller than any in the restored area and lacked any important construction on its flat top. Someone had cleared a path up the side of it, and Lori began to climb slowly, creeping on all fours like an animal; the stones were too narrow and badly spaced for her to stand erect. All her senses were alert for any movement or sound from within, but there was nothing.

She reached the top and paused to look around. Just as before, a stone had been moved in the center of the flat area, and a dim light shone up from below. Creeping over to it to look in, she again saw the stone steps leading down, and she knew that if she went down the steps she would confront Erik's murderer.

She paused there on the top step, her heart pounding. Now she realized how foolish it had been to come here alone—but what else could she have done? If she had waited, the opportunity to learn the truth might have been lost forever. A clammy sweat broke out over her body, and she began to tremble. Suppose he caught her again and left her there in the tomb in the total dark—she didn't think she could bear it a second time. She would go mad. She would die of sheer terror.

Her one thought at that moment was that she

should turn and get away from there as fast as she could, go away with Brian and forget the whole business. She was actually starting to retreat when an unidentified sound from below broke into her moment of panic. Of course she had to go on!

Slowly she crept down the stairs toward the bend, knowing that when she reached that point she could see the rest of the way. The stones felt rough and cold against her hand as she pressed it against the wall to keep from stumbling. This time she did not intend to fall and knock herself out.

When she reached the bend, she paused, gazing down. It was all so much the same as what had happened before that she had a queer sense of déjà vu. There was the lantern on the stone floor sending out its dull glow, and there, in an archway, was the robed figure—only this time there was only one person there, and what had been a bloody body was now only a pile of bones. Slowly the robed figure moved over to that ghastly pile and began collecting and stuffing the bones into a plastic garbage bag.

Lori looked around the interior of the pyramid, which was a small room, probably no more than ten feet in diameter, and roughly circular in shape. Against the far side was an alcove, which contained the carefully arranged bones of an ancient skeleton —the high priest, Tzab?—who was buried there, surrounded by a ring of something that she remembered vaguely as witchcraft stones. At his feet was the skeleton of a small animal, probably a dog, put there to keep him company in the hereafter. Some distance away was a Chac-Mool, just a small one, which must have been brought there from the upper platform. Now she knew why the figure always caused her such unease. Her subconscious must have remembered seeing it down there.

And on the floor, propped against the small stone altar, was a magnificent sheet-gold disk bearing the image of the great Kukulcan, the Feathered Serpent —encircled by smaller figures of warriors, animals, and birds. The last time she had seen it, it had lain beside Erik's still body.

She knew about those disks, had even seen one in the Peabody museum. The Mayans had no gold of their own but had made such disks from crumpled balls of gold taken from the Sacred Spring, where they had been thrown as offerings by the faithful who came long distances to pay homage to their gods. The thought of the disk's value staggered the mind. What Mr. V. had offered to pay was only a fraction of its real worth today.

All the memories were crowding back now. She knew now that she had never seen the face of the hooded figure. After one horrified glimpse of Erik's bloody body, she had pitched headfirst down the remaining steps, hitting her head on a sharp corner at the bottom.

She remembered that she had awakened a little later, just as she did in the nightmares—awakened to total darkness, knowing that somewhere nearby lay that ghastly thing that had been Erik. Now she could remember her frantic crawling around in the darkness, searching for some way of escape, anything to get away from what was lying there. She had knocked over the lantern, which had been extinguished, and climbed up the stairs only to find the entrance blocked by a solid mass of stone, with no way to open it. She had climbed back down and wandered around the tomb, searching, searching, trying to avoid both the newly dead Erik and the long-dead priest. Then, to her incredible relief, she had fumbled into an opening in the side of the tomb. Concealed behind a stone urn, it led into a tunnel. She had crawled for what seemed like miles until she had finally emerged into a cave, and from there out onto a ledge above the second *cenote*. By then dawn was breaking so she could see where she was.

She had known the area well, having been there with her father as well as alone, so she had climbed the cliff, made her way along the path to the ruins, and finally out onto the road. By then her mind had blocked out a good deal of it, retaining only a confused memory of a bloody Erik and a feathered serpent. . . .

Lori brought her mind back from its wandering

through the past and gazed again at the figure busily shoving Erik's remains into the sack. She must have made some slight sound at this point, because the hooded figure whirled toward her, the hood falling back from its face. Lori gazed down in utter astonishment.

CHAPTER THIRTEEN

"Mrs. Armstrong!" Lori exclaimed. "What are you doing here?"

The woman gave an annoyed shrug. "Oh, Lori! Why did you have to follow me here? After all the work I've gone through to discourage you—you just wouldn't give up, would you?"

Astonishment was giving place to a cold feeling of dismay. Surely Mrs. Armstrong—but no! It was impossible. "What do you mean?" Lori asked. "Are you the one who's been doing all those things to frighten me?"

"Yes, dear, I'm afraid so. I didn't actually want to harm you, you know. I just wanted to discourage

161

you. But you wouldn't discourage." She picked up Erik's skull and eyed it sadly.

Lori felt the hysterical urge to cry, "Alas, poor Erik, I knew him, Horatio," but Mrs. Armstrong spoke instead.

"Poor boy, a pity he had to die so young, but it was his own fault. Greed, you know. It's a dangerous emotion."

Lori came closer, regarding Mrs. Armstrong with horrified fascination. "You—you were here that night?"

"Unfortunately, yes. We never should have become involved in such an unsavory affair."

"But you weren't the one I saw leading Erik to the pyramid."

"No, that was my husband. I was already here, hiding behind the altar. We were afraid, you see, that Erik might try something funny. Which he did, of course. So I wore this monk's costume and death mask—I was going to pop out and scare him if he tried anything. He was awfully nervous about coming down here anyway, and I thought if he thought I was the ghost of the dead priest, he'd panic and run away. But it didn't quite work out that way."

"Mrs. Armstrong," Lori said, "would you mind explaining the whole thing—from the beginning?"

"Why, no. I guess you're entitled to know." She stuck Erik's head in the sack with the rest of him. "It all began a long time ago. My husband, Ben, and I used to be in vaudeville. He was a magician, very clever. Used to saw me in half." She sighed, remembering the good old days. "Then vaudeville died, so we got up a mind-reading act we did in nightclubs. I won't bore you with our methods, but we were very effective. That kept us going for quite a while. Ben really got interested in the metaphysical during this period; he read all sorts of books, especially about spiritualism. He was interested in archaeology too, the old Egyptian and Mayan stuff. It sort of tied in, I guess.

"Anyway, we got a bit tired traveling around all the time, so Ben got the idea of trying the medium business, so we could stay in one place. He thought I'd be a natural for it. We found a nice little apartment in Lake Worth and got me set up as a medium. He knew all about it, and we built up quite a nice little business. Because of Ben's interest in archaeology, he had me use a Mayan priest for a control. Sort of struck his fancy." She glanced over at the neatly arranged skeleton nearby. "Wouldn't it be funny if this one's name really was Tzab? He got to be so real to me, I sort of believed in him myself. And sometimes it seems to me the spirits really are talking—"

"What about the séance you held the other night?" Lori asked. "The things you said seemed to be authentic enough to upset some of us, at any rate."

"I told you I was good," she replied complacently. "It isn't hard when you know how. Julian had told me about his nightmares, of course. Once when Dr. Parker was out, I went into his cottage and found a mushy letter from some girlfriend. I knew that his wife had died a few years ago, and apparently he'd taken up with someone a lot younger.

"As for Miss Gregory—she confided to me once that she'd had an illegitimate baby when she was very young—a little girl who died when she was only four."

"Did you know about the song?" Lori asked.

"Twinkle, twinkle? No, that was odd, wasn't it. It just sort of came to me while I was talking. Seemed to strike a nerve, too, because Miss Gregory got all upset. Of course all that about your father was to throw you off thinking Erik was dead. I thought if I could convince you he was still alive, you'd leave. What I said about the would-be murderer being in the room— Oh, I don't know—it just seemed an effective exit line.

"But to get back to my life story—we had a friend in the same apartment building who traveled a lot, and she always laughed about how easy it was for senior citizens, especially if they were with a tour group, to get through customs in Miami. She said the inspectors hardly ever looked in their bags, just pushed them on through. She said she ought to take up smuggling.

"Well, Ben got to thinking about that. He'd read a lot about artifacts, how valuable they were, so he said, 'Let's go down to the Yucatán and look around.' So that's what we did. We visited a lot of ruins, including Chichén Itzá, and Ben was crazy about them. The next year we came here and stayed a month, and he inquired around. Picked up a few things here and there, took them home, and sold them to a dealer we heard about. Nothing to it.

"Of course one thing always leads to another, and he kept hoping for something major to turn up that would keep us in luxury for the rest of our lives. By chance he found a fellow here at the hotel, one of the Mexican yard men, who had Mayan ancestors and knew all about the old religion and the local ruins. He said there was a pyramid back in the jungle, and he knew the secret of opening it. Said somebody must have hidden a cache of stuff there in the past from the Well of Sacrifice. Divers brought up all kinds of things, you know. We got a lot of things from him. But he wouldn't tell us where the pyramid was.

"Well, now we come to the spring twelve years ago, when the archeologists were working here and you came down to visit your father. We were here, staying in the hotel because the workers had all the cabins. Somehow Erik got wind of the fact that we had a source of good artifacts, so he came to us. He said he knew of a buyer—a multimillionaire who would pay a fortune for something really good. He asked if we knew of anything like that. So we asked our Mexican, and he hemmed and hawed a bit and finally admitted there was one really good thing in the pyramid."

"The gold disk!" Lori exclaimed.

"Right. But the trouble was that the man—his name was Pedro—said that there was a curse on it and that anybody who tried to remove it from the tomb would die. So, of course, he wouldn't touch it."

"How did he know there was a curse on it?"

Mrs. Armstrong shrugged. "I don't know. He just said his grandfather had told him, and his grandfather before him. Very ancient curse. The other artifacts were okay, they'd been hidden in the tomb more recently, but not the disk. That had been put in there with the body of the priest to protect him or something, and touching it was a no-no.

"Well, we worked on him for a long time, and finally he agreed to take Ben into the pyramid to see it. Ben went there with him, and Pedro even showed him how to open the pyramid. It isn't hard, just tricky. You have to know which stone to press on."

"Can it be opened from the inside too?" Lori asked, remembering her own frantic efforts.

"Yes, there's a hidden lever. But unless you knew where it was, you probably couldn't find it. He showed Ben the disk—it used to sit on a ledge above Tzab's bones—and Ben took a picture of it. This he showed to Erik, who in turn showed it to the millionaire collector on the yacht, who got terribly excited about it. He offered Erik three hundred fifty thousand dollars for it."

"It's worth a lot more," Lori pointed out.

"Probably, but just look at it, Lori." She gestured toward the disk, glittering in the lamplight. "How could you smuggle a big thing like that out of Mexico? Up to then we'd taken back only little things that could be tucked neatly into a suitcase. And how would you know who to sell it to if you did get it out? Our dealer wouldn't have handled anything like that. No, our only hope was the man on the yacht."

"Mr. V.," Lori murmured.

"Yes. I know that you and Brian visited him the other day. Does he still want the disk?"

"Very much."

"Good. So Erik told Ben to bring him the disk and they could go together to the yacht with it and split the proceeds. Now Ben had been reading up on all that old stuff—and would you believe, he was actually afraid to remove the disk?"

"He thought he would drop dead if he touched it?" Lori asked.

"Something like that. He said he'd take Erik in and let him get it."

"Erik wasn't afraid of it?"

"I think he was, sort of, but the desire to get hold of all that money was stronger. He didn't want to go back to college, and Mr. V. had promised to let him go along to South America."

"So that's what I saw that night—your husband leading Erik to the pyramid."

"Right. But we didn't trust Erik, so I went on ahead with my costume and hid over there"—she nodded toward the altar—"and waited to see what would happen. Well, they came, and Erik climbed up and grabbed the disk first thing. He was so eager that he was trembling all over and his eyes were shining in a queer way—you know, the way a dog's eyes shine when it's preparing to kill something."

"You think Erik was planning to—to kill your husband?" Lori said in disbelief. Erik had always seemed so harmless—

"There's no doubt about it! First thing he did after getting down the disk was to pull out a gun—some sort of little pistol—and order Ben to stand against the wall with his hands over his head. Ben did as he was told, naturally, and I saw Erik lift the pistol and point it at Ben. I knew he was going to shoot my Ben, and believe me I saw red. There was that sacrificial knife right there on the altar— Well, I forgot about scaring Erik. A man pointing a gun doesn't scare too easily anyway, I guess. I just stood up, grabbed that knife, and threw it—all in one motion."

"You could throw it accurately at that distance?"

"Oh, yes. One year we toured the South doing our magic act with a little circus, and we got real chummy with the knife thrower. Just for fun we had him give us lessons, and we both got pretty good at it. It's not that difficult. Of course I'm out of practice now, but if I'd wanted to hit you there by that lake a few hours ago, I wouldn't have missed. I've never wanted to really hurt you, Lori. I like you."

"Thanks," she said dryly. "And that's when I heard Erik yell?"

"Yes, he let out an awful screech when the knife

hit him. He fell, dropping the gun and the disk beside him. The gun's probably still here." She stirred around in the remaining bones and came up with a pistol. "Yes, here it is. The knife's there too. I have to get rid of that along with the bones, I suppose."

"But go on, what did you do then?"

"Ben was standing there like he was petrified, and I walked over to Erik to see if he was dead. I pulled the knife out, thinking I might need to use it again if he wasn't—and that was when you came tumbling down the stairs. I never did know if you got a good look at me or not."

"I didn't. All I remember is seeing a figure with a hood."

"So you were unconscious and Erik was dead. Ben said we had to get out of there fast—just close up the tomb and hope nobody ever found it. So that's what we did. I wanted to take the disk and sell it to Mr. V. ourselves, but Ben wouldn't let me. He said it really was cursed and tainted with fresh blood. Well, that was true enough. It did have blood on it from Erik. I hated to leave it, but Ben wouldn't let me touch it. He was sort of hysterical by then. He never did like violence, my Ben." Mrs. Armstrong sighed.

"But what about me? Did you just decide to leave me there?"

"What else could we do? You had seen me commit a murder. Anyway, Ben said you were dead too. So we turned off the lantern, hustled out, and closed up the tomb. With a little luck, we figured nobody would open it again until after we were dead."

"Didn't you think anyone would come looking for me?"

"Yes, but we didn't think you'd be missed until morning, and nobody knew about the pyramid except us."

"And Pedro."

"Oh, he wouldn't talk. He was too scared of being arrested for pilfering the tomb, and he knew Julian's dad would fire him if he found out. Believe me, we were scared silly when you were found the next morning, but fortunately you didn't seem to remember anything. Ben had gone back right away and cut a lot of bushes and stuff to cover up the entrance to the path, so nobody was able to find it. Then he took Erik's car with all his stuff in it—Erik had been all ready to leave as soon as he got back, with the note on the table and everything—and drove it to Cancun and abandoned it near the dock. Then he took the early-morning bus back to Chichén Itaź, and nobody even knew he'd been gone, except me."

"It certainly worked out well for you," Lori said, still not quite believing what she was hearing, "except that you didn't get any money."

"Oh, that was all right. We decided a life of crime wasn't worth all the worry it caused, so we left right away and have never been back since. Until now, of course."

"Why did you come back now?"

"It was that notice in the paper about them going to start working on the ruins again, restoring a new area. Ben saw that and he panicked. He said they'd find the pyramid for sure, and it still had Erik's body in it, not to mention the knife with my fingerprints on it. It scared him so that he had a stroke; he's been in the hospital for quite a while. They say he'll probably have to go into a nursing home for a couple of months or more, maybe for good, when he gets out, depending on what progress he makes. But he was still fretting about the pyramid, and I knew he wouldn't improve until I did something about it. So I said I'd come back and find it and destroy the evidence of any crime.

"Then, when I got here, I couldn't find the pyramid! I hunted and hunted, but the path has really grown shut now, and I wasn't exactly sure where it had been after all this time. I was desperate. Finally I realized I'd never find it alone, that I'd have to contact Pedro again. I knew he was distantly related to Julian and had worked here then, so I asked Julian where he was. He said that Pedro still worked for him but was on vacation and had gone to Miami to visit his aunt.

"He told me when he'd be back, so I settled down to wait for him. I called Ben every night to keep him informed, and he agreed that was best. Pedro got home yesterday, so right away I asked him to find the path and clear it for me. I offered him a huge reward—said this time I was going to get the disk and sell it, because the man on the yacht was back."

"Didn't he wonder why you hadn't taken it the first time?"

"No, because in order to keep him away from the pyramid in the future, Ben had told him that we were all attacked by evil spirits in the tomb and had to run away. I told Pedro now that I had found a very strong magic talisman that would keep the bad spirits away. I showed him one of those weird-looking tikis from New Zealand that I'd picked up once, and he believed that it must have magic powers. So he found the path—he said there was a mark on a tree at the beginning of it—and cleared it with a machete, enough for me to get through."

"But you're not really going to take the disk, are you?" Lori asked.

"Of course I am! As soon as Brian told me about your visit with Mr. V., I decided I'd not only get rid of the evidence, but take the disk as well. I'm going to need all the money I can get to keep Ben in a good nursing home for a while."

"But didn't he tell you not to touch it?" Lori gave the glittering object a fearful glance. It had already caused Erik's death. Who would be next?

"Of course. That was the last thing he said to me: 'Leave that cursed disk alone, baby!' But I don't always do what I'm told, you know." She gave Lori an impish grin.

"And all along you were the one doing all those things to me?"

"I just wanted to make you go away," she said indignantly. "You showed up at the wrong time—while I was waiting for Pedro to come back. You had been to the pyramid—I couldn't have you messing around and maybe finding it and getting it opened before I had a chance to take Erik out. So I thought I'd scare you off."

"I suppose you heard what I said to Julian the night I got here."

"Yes, but I already knew you were coming. Julian told me. He thought I'd be interested because I was here when you were here before. That's why I was sitting in the lobby."

"So you looked in my window with the death mask on."

"Yes, and pulled the bag over your head when you came out to see what was out there. I wasn't trying to kill you. I pulled it off again as soon as you fainted."

"I thought it was a man."

"I'm very strong. And I was wearing trousers and a man's jacket."

"But it couldn't have been you at the Sacred Spring," Lori protested. "Brian took a picture—"

"That was me all right," she said complacently. "The fat lady in the red wig. I'm a master at disguising myself and changing my voice."

"When did Pedro get the path opened up?"

"Earlier today—or I should say, yesterday. I was going to go to the pyramid first thing in the morning—I don't like the jungle at night. But then when I listened outside your window tonight, I heard you say you were going to the police, so I thought I'd better not lose any time. It's unfortunate that you followed me here. I thought I could get the disk and Erik out of here and be on my way to the yacht long before you came with the police."

Lori didn't like the sound of that word, "unfortunate." "But I did follow you," she said, "so now what?"

"I never wanted it to come to this, but you leave me no choice. I guess it's you or me, baby, as they said in the old flicks." The little gun was raised, pointing at her. Lori stared at it.

"It's been here untouched for twelve years," Lori said through dry lips. "It won't fire."

"Want to bet? It's nice and dry in here. No rust."

"But—what are you going to do, Mrs. Armstrong? Just shoot me and leave me here?"

"I can't do that, dear. I came here to remove Erik, so I can't leave you instead. No, you must both leave, but you can go out under your own power. I'll just close up the pyramid so nobody will follow us, and we'll go out the back way—the route you must have used to escape when we left you here."

"If you know about that, why didn't you come here

that way in the first place, remove Erik and the disk, and go? Why wait for Pedro to cut you a path?"

"Because I didn't know until after Pedro had cut me the path. I told him then that I had always been puzzled as to how you had gotten out of the pyramid, and he said you must have found the back tunnel. I asked him why he didn't tell me about it instead of going to so much work, and he said that was the priest's way of coming and going so he could appear or disappear suddenly and amaze the worshipers. He said it was sacred and forbidden to anyone else."

"A curse on it, I suppose. But I used it, and nothing happened to me."

"Of course not. If I believed that, would I be using it? And would I be removing the sacred disk?" She shoved the last of the bones into her bag and added the sacrificial dagger. "There now. Erik's all ready. You wait here while I go up and close the pyramid. If anyone had followed you, he'd be here by now, but I don't want to take any chances."

She started to back up the stairs, one step at a time, sitting down facing Lori with the gun pointed toward her. The situation was so ridiculous Lori almost felt like giggling—except that it was truly dangerous. Mrs. Armstrong must be quite mad, Lori thought, and the best thing to do would be to humor her until she was out of the pyramid. Then she'd have to make a break for it. Would a gun fire after twelve years? She had no idea, but she didn't particularly want to find out.

As she worked her way up the steps, Mrs. Armstrong kept talking. "The people who lived in the deserted village used to come here to worship long after it was outlawed by the Spaniards," she said. "Pedro told us all about it. They had a priest and held their ceremonies. Very secret. That's why they brought the Chac-Mool down here. It used to be on top, where the ceremonies should be held. He thought they might even have made human sacrifices. The man who is buried here was from the older days. It must have been one of those people who hid the artifacts Pedro used to bring us from here. They're all gone now. Only the disk remains."

She disappeared around the bend. "Don't try to rush me, dear," she called down, "because I still have the gun ready and I won't hesitate to shoot."

Lori decided to stay where she was. Her chances would be better outside. In a moment she heard a dull thud as the opening stone fell into place, and then Mrs. Armstrong came scooting back down.

She picked up the sack and handed it to Lori. "You carry Erik, dear, and I'll bring the disk. It isn't as heavy as it looks, because it's so thin. You go first. I'll be right behind you with the gun, so please don't try anything."

Lori cleared away the debris piled in front of the opening and saw a dark hole, no more than three feet high. She vaguely remembered crawling for some distance before she was able to stand upright.

"We'll leave the lantern burning," Mrs. Armstrong decided. "It will give us light for a little way. It's too big to carry when we have so many other things."

Lori started crawling along the tunnel, dragging the sack beside her. She didn't like the sounds the bones made.

"What are you going to do with the sack when we get out?" she asked Mrs. Armstrong, who was panting along behind her, having a bit of difficulty with the long robe.

"Oh, I guess I'll throw it in the *cenote*. That's one reason I decided to use this exit. I'll just put a stone in the bag with him and sink it. Also, this way is safer, in case anyone comes along the path. No one ever goes to the *cenote* at night."

Lori supposed that she would also be sunk in the well, after being shot, but she really didn't care to discuss it. The whole situation seemed so totally unreal, like a weird nightmare. Here she was, crawling along a dark tunnel, carrying the bones of an old acquaintance, and probably heading for her own untimely doom. Perhaps she would never see Brian again. But she had to! It couldn't end like this.

It was very dark in the tunnel, but there was no place to go except to keep crawling forward in this seemingly interminable nightmare. Finally, to Lori's great relief, she was able to stand up, and now she moved more cautiously, one hand trailing along the stone wall for guidance. She could hear Mrs. Armstrong panting along behind her.

Now she came to an opening that she remembered as leading into the dead-end crevice where she had hidden from what she had believed to be her enemy. That meant it was not much farther to the cave and the *cenote*. It also meant that in a few more minutes Mrs. Armstrong intended to shoot her and toss her into the spring along with Erik's bones. What was she going to do about it?

She would be the first one out of the cave. She could throw the sack at Mrs. Armstrong and make a dash for it, hoping that the woman wasn't as good a marksman with a gun as she was with a knife. Or she could attack her and try to get the gun away from her—possibly getting shot in the process. Or she could do nothing and pray that the gun would no longer fire.

It was hard to believe that Mrs. Armstrong would actually shoot her, and yet—she was such a weird woman, and apparently she would stop at nothing to protect her Ben. And she seemed to think she had to sell the disk to Mr. V. and get back to take care of her husband, no matter what she had to do to get there. Lori decided to make one more attempt to reason with the woman.

"Mrs. Armstrong," she said over her shoulder, "you know that when you killed Erik it was really self-defense. I don't think you would be convicted of murder. But if you kill me now, that would be cold-blooded, first-degree murder, and you would go to prison. Why don't you just leave the disk here, and we'll both go home? We can still throw Erik's bones into the *cenote,* if you like, and I won't tell anyone about this."

"I'm not leaving the disk here after all the trouble I've gone to," she replied indignantly. "I want to get the money so I can take care of Ben."

"Okay, then keep the disk if you like—but it isn't necessary to shoot me. I promise not to tell anyone about it."

Mrs. Armstrong was silent a few moments, apparently thinking it over; then she replied, "I'd like to trust you, Lori, but I can't. It would make you an accomplice in Erik's death if you helped me get rid of the evidence, and I can't believe you'd do something like that. You're too ethical. I know your type. I'm not ethical at all. I've always done what I had to do to get along. And that includes killing someone if necessary. And I'm afraid it is necessary to kill you, because if I don't, you'll talk, no matter what you say now, and then I won't be able to go home and take care of Ben. I *have* to get home to him, don't you see? There's no one but me to take care of him."

With a sick feeling in the pit of her stomach, Lori realized that the woman was beyond reason or logic. Only one thing had any reality for her and that was doing what was best for Ben. The only recourse Lori had left was to revert to one of her original choices, whatever seemed most feasible when the moment of confrontation arrived. Of course the gun might not fire, but she didn't know enough about firearms to take a chance on it.

She could see a dim glimmer of light ahead now, which was moonlight shining in the entrance to the cave. She hesitated, and Mrs. Armstrong prodded her in the back with the gun.

"Go on," she commanded. "We're almost there now. Don't worry, dear. Dying isn't anything much, and you'll soon be on the other side with all those nice people who have gone before. Won't you be happy to see your father again?"

"But it was all fake," Lori said stiffly. "I thought you didn't really believe in such things."

"Oh, I didn't say that. I just said we fake the contact with them. And once in a great while someone really does seem to get through. Of course I believe there are spirits out there. I wouldn't be very convincing in my job if I didn't."

Now they were in the cave, bathed in an eerie glow of moonlight. Lori could hear the water lapping gently far below and hear the cries of night birds out in the jungle. At least it was a relief to be out of the darkness of the tunnel. They went on out to the ledge above the *cenote*.

"Pick up one of those rocks," Mrs. Armstrong ordered, pointing to a few loose ones that had fallen down from the cliffs above. "Put it into the sack with Erik. That's it. He needs to be weighted down properly, so he'll sink." After placing the disk carefully on the ledge, she fished a short length of rope out of the pocket of her capacious robe. "Now, tie it up, then throw it in. You may say a few words in his memory, if you like."

This was getting crazier by the minute, Lori thought. She kneeled, tied up the sack, and dropped it gently over the edge. She couldn't think of anything to say. Apparently he had been a crook and a would-be murderer. "Good-bye, Erik," she murmured. "Rest in peace."

"That was nice," Mrs. Armstrong said. "Now stay as you are, dear, kneeling there by the edge. I'm going to shoot you and push you right over to join Erik. The *cenote* is very deep, and the bottom is covered with a thick layer of muck. Nobody dives here, because no treasure was ever thrown in; it was purely for drinking water. I doubt that either of you will ever be found. There would be no reason for looking here."

All the ideas Lori had had seemed useless now, when she was caught in such an awkward position. Only one thing remained to be done—she had to go over into the water before the woman had time to fire, and trust that Mrs. Armstrong couldn't see her down there in the dark. Mrs. Armstrong was raising the weapon, holding it with both hands, pointing at Lori's head. Lori threw herself flat onto the ledge, preparing to roll over the edge.

At the same moment a frenzy of barking broke

out at the top of the path leading down from the rim of the *cenote,* and a small figure, followed by two larger ones, came hurtling down. It all happened so quickly, Lori didn't have time to take in what was happening. The small creature leaped on Mrs. Armstrong in a frenzy of greeting; the woman cried out in surprise, tried to back off from the men who were running toward her, caught her foot on the disk, which she had placed behind her, and fell backward off the ledge into the *cenote.*

The woman's last, terrible scream was vibrating in her ears when Lori felt herself being picked up and clutched frantically to Brian's chest.

"Lori!" he cried. "Thank God we made it in time! What possessed you to go off alone after that woman?"

"I didn't have time to wake you," she protested, clinging to him, aware that she was trembling violently from shock.

The other man was slipping off his shoes. Then he dove over the edge after Mrs. Armstrong.

"Who was that?" Lori asked feebly. "And what are you doing here?"

"That's your pal Perez," Brian told her.

"But how did you get here—like the cavalry to the rescue or something?"

"You can thank Chang for that." They both looked at the little dog that was standing at the edge of the ledge, looking down and uttering pitiful little whimpers. "He woke me up. Apparently he got out again and was trying to follow his mistress, but he couldn't get through the gate. I heard him barking and carrying on out in back, so I got up to see what was the matter. I could see he wanted me to let him onto the path. First I checked Mrs. Armstrong's cottage — she wasn't there. Then I checked yours, and you weren't there, either. I panicked then, so I decided to let the dog through the gate and follow him."

"How did Perez get into the act?"

"Oh, he was out there too — watching Max's cottage. So when he heard all the racket he came over and decided to join me. He was bored, I guess. I can't believe that nice little old lady was going to shoot you! You'll have to give me the whole story."

"I will, but first finish yours. You went into the jungle — so how on earth did you end up here? I know the pyramid was closed, so unless you knew how to open it, you couldn't have come that way. Anyway, you didn't come out through the cave, you were up above."

"The dog led us to the pyramid — who opened up the path? Anyway, we got there, and Chang went up on top and fussed around, but Perez and I couldn't figure how to open the thing. Then Chang ran down again, we followed, and he led us to a sort of path going off into the jungle. Not the newly opened one we'd come in on, but an old one — it looked like a wild-pig trail or something. It came out up there where you saw us appear. Fortunately Perez carried a flashlight, so we could see where we were going. The dog hurtled down to Mrs. Armstrong, we followed, and you know the rest."

Just then there was a shout from the water, and they both peered down. They could just make out Perez's head sticking out, and another beside him.

"I've got her!" he shouted. "But I think she's dead. Looks like she hit her head on a jagged rock on the way down. The cliff is too steep to climb out with her. Go back to the hotel for help—have them bring a rope."

"Will you be all right?" Lori shouted down to him.

"Yes, I'm hanging on to a projecting rock here. I'll be all right. But hurry!"

Lori and Brian didn't waste any more time. They climbed the path to the top of the *cenote* and hurried off along the path back to the ruins. On the way, Lori recounted everything that Mrs. Armstrong had told her.

"What a story!" Brian said when she'd finished. "And so the sacred disk struck again! Maybe the curse really is true."

"Only in that the greed for riches often brings about man's downfall," Lori said soberly. "Oh, Brian—that poor, deluded woman! Who will look after Ben now?"

"I don't know. The poor guy—he warned her not to touch the disk. You see what happens to wives who don't listen to their husbands!"

"I never dreamed she was mixed up in this. I

knew it was a man who took Erik into the jungle, and that threw me off. I rather suspected Julian."

"Why Julian?"

"Because he's such a strange man, and he does have Mayan blood. I thought he might feel it his duty to guard the sacred disk and not let anyone steal it. And, of course, he's been here all along."

"True, but I rather fancied pretty-boy Max myself. He could have been one of the students."

Lori sighed. "You know, Brian, I keep wondering—would that gun really have gone off? I don't know enough about them to know if it could after twelve years."

"Neither do I," he admitted. "Well, it's at the bottom of the *cenote* now—along with Erik—so we'll never know, will we?"

A few days later they were in Brian's car, headed for the airport. They had coped with the police, the paparazzi, frantic calls from parents, hordes of tourists, and all the rest that went with a rather spectacular news story. Now it was over, and they could get on with their lives.

The gold disk had been sent to the museum in Mexico City, and so far nobody had dropped dead from handling it. The authorities were still holding Mrs. Armstrong's body; Max had returned to his Jane. And now Lori and Brian were going to fly to California to see his parents, then to Chicago to get married, and finally home to Oregon.

Brian gave Lori a tender, rather rueful glance as the fields of sisal sped by.

"Are you quite sure, love," he asked, "that you can stand to settle in such an out-of-the-way little town? Because I could move my business to Chicago if—"

"Forget it," she interrupted. "I've always wanted to live by the ocean. And you did say it's within easy commuting distance of Portland. I understand they've got a very good orchestra there. It will all work out. At the moment, after all we've gone through, all I want to do is settle down and lead a quiet, uneventful life."

"Ha!" he said. "Knowing you, somehow I doubt that!"

He reached over and took her hand, and she smiled a little secret smile as she gazed off into the future.